Threads

by

Patsy Brookshire

To Dede,
enjoy the mist on
your face, Love,
Patsy B.
7-14-06

Threads
© 2006 by Patsy Brookshire

Published by Patsy Brookshire
P.O. Box 1805
Newport, OR 97366

Manufactured in the United States of America by Newport LAZERQUICK
in conjunction with Dancing Moon Press.

Book Design: Newport LAZERQUICK
Cover Design: Andrew E. Cier

ISBN: 978-1-892076-27-4

Library of Congress Control Number: 2006906074

Brookshire, Patsy
Threads
1. Title;
2. Northwest Author;
3. Pacific Northwest Fiction

FIRST EDITION
July 2006

Dedication

To Bob Chaney

*Thank you for reading Threads, supporting, encouraging,
and teaching me how to change a tire
in case I should ever need to.*

1. I Know You're Busy, But...

It's unnerving to realize that I am not completely in charge of my future, that the past events and decisions made by another person can then wriggle their way into my life, affecting what I do today, and, what I do tomorrow. Such as the effect of these old, yellowed letters of Aunt Sophie's. You wouldn't think the words of a 14-year-old boy could spur me to spending my evenings at this typewriter, compelled to catching quickly the story of a family, most of whose members are long dead. I would much rather be out taking pictures or looking at the full moon with Roger, but, as Aunt Sophie used to say, "First things first, Annie!" Agitating.

It's midwinter now and the rain of the last week has let up to just a soft dripping from the eve over my bedroom window to the flower bed below, pooling in the dirt under the cedar chips. The fresh smell through the open window is a pleasant accompaniment to the annoying hum of this old typewriter. My entrance into the story I have to tell began on quite another day, just prior to the unusually warm Labor Day weekend of last Fall.

I had dropped by Aunt Sophie's place for just a few minutes after work to see if there was anything she needed before I left for the holiday. The old gal threw me a curve, she asked me to spend the whole weekend with her. When I reluctantly agreed I never intended to remain the full three days.

I had loosely arranged to spend Sunday and Monday nights in the mountains with Len. Len. Another memory, but at the time he was very current and, I thought, was my future. By the stream by day and the cabin fire by night we would have 'A wonderful experience', 'Get to know each other better', and, I hoped, clear up some difficulties in our relationship.

And then, Aunt Sophie, with her clear-eyed logic, said, "Annie, you're 22 and soon will be tied down with this Len fellow," (she could never just say, "Len") "and won't have time for your old auntie. You'll be busy with a house, and kids, and what all, and before you know it I'll be gone." She knew I hated any references to her age, or death, and that it was an effective way to get to me.

"Of course, I know you're busy, and you young people do have your own lives to live...." I brushed that aside - even though I agreed with her. "But I found a late patch of blackberries back in the woods yesterday, and, you know, what with my hip and all, I didn't get any jam or pies put up this year, and I just thought, wouldn't it be nice if Annie and I could do those up together!" She was pulling all my strings now. "Remember when you were just little and weren't much more than a bother, and how you loved to help me?"

So I told her I'd see if I couldn't work something out, some time in, but I couldn't promise more than to see if I could get off work early at the photo shop. That would give us Friday afternoon and all Saturday but I already had, "plans for Sunday and Monday."

She seemed happy at that and I went home to my apartment not thinking much more about it. But late that night, after having suffered through an inane TV program while I waited, in vain, for Len (sensitive, emotional, black-haired, black-eyed Len whom I planned to marry in the spring) to call, I'd gone to bed, and instead of the sleep I craved, started thinking about my aunt.

Aunt Sophie was nearing 80. The age difference had never mattered, she'd always been my best friend, the one who taught me how to dress: "Be neat, Annie. Simple, but always put a little thought into your clothes, a little flair!"

She analyzed my shape: "You're going to be tall. You'll be able to wear just about anything - but stay away from frills, they'll just make you look silly. With that blond hair of your mother's, and your dad's sweet mouth you don't need to look any ... well, you're something enough."

She undertook to study my character: "You're going to make mistakes," she told me one afternoon as she held me to her soft chest and patted me on the back. I'd come home heartsick because I'd told a secret a friend had trusted me not to tell, and the friend had found me out. I was sad, and embarrassed. "But use them to improve yourself!"

"Here," she took her hankie, (white lace, it was) from where she always carried it in the belt of her housedress, and wiped my eyes with the so-soft cloth. Her hands were old even then, lightly dusted with brown spots. Purple veins from her wrists traced down the fingers of her sturdy hands. Long, wide hands, worker hands. Laying her face against my wet cheek, she said, "Dear Annie," and kissed me quickly.

"Friendship is so fragile, but, somebody will trust you again, and, next time you will do better! I have faith in you!" She said this firmly, so that I believed her.

With Aunt Sophie shaping me like a tender young pear tree, pruning here and there, and propping up my fragile limbs, I grew strong enough to stand up on my own, and felt that I could weather any storms.

She was old-fashioned but she was the only one who took the time to care, to notice me.

I owed her a lot.

I loved her deeply.

2. Elm Branches

reat Aunt Sophie was my father's mother's, sister. She never married so was sometimes referred to as, "Poor Aunt Sophie," at least by the more charitable members of the Elm family. This was a short list: two cousins of mine who left Oregon to move to far-away New York at a young age, to return to the bosom of the family in their late forties, long after Aunt Sophie's prime years. Someone else in the family, I remember Great Uncle Zack in particular, would snort, and say, "Poor Aunt Sophie my eye! I wish I could have got somebody to support me the way she did!"

Aunt Sophie earned her keep. She lived with almost everyone in the family at one time or other and made a quilt for each of them. The quilts were personalized, depicting something close to the receiver's heart. They were beautiful.

Other than the New York cousins and myself, my Uncle Boyd was the only other relative who spoke up in his Aunt's defense, and he did so from the distance of Washington, D.C. He provided her with the home she had lived in since she was in her fifties.

The Elm family had many branches (sorry, it's a family joke). Grandma Mandy and Great Aunt Sophie, known to us simply as Aunt Sophie, had three brothers and three other sisters. Two of the brothers, Zack and Trevor, never married.

Trevor never had a chance. In late 1917, at age seventeen, he went off enthusiastically to join the "war to end all wars" but by the spring of 1918 he was dead, shot, it was said, by a French housewife. The full story was never known and the family didn't seek details, it being enough coping with the fact that Trevor had been dispatched by an ally. But it wasn't hard to figure out - Trevor had been of a terror at home with a number of neighboring women and girls, so they had reason not to look or question too closely.

Scandal was abhorred by the Elms. 'Ignore the unpleasant or uncomfortable' was almost a family motto. The grief this caused can never be measured, certainly Aunt Sophie paid a high price to maintain it.

Trevor's death shocked the family but particularly left its mark on his younger brothers, especially Zack who took it bitterly. Ever afterwards affection for anyone or anything was tempered with a grim reserve. He must have secretly admired Trevor's rough reputation but didn't have the guts to carry it off, just enough to be dangerous when thwarted.

He remained highly visible within the family circle, passionately unmarried and constantly voicing his contempt and distrust of women, mining his sisters' lives for mistakes to use as evidence of his rightness, while at the same time borrowing money from them to fill in the gaps left from the many dollars spent on liquor and trifles towards his latest bar mate.

The other brother, my Great Uncle Willie, married young but only had two children (the New York cousins), before he was killed in a logging accident in 1925. His wife sold their small farm, took the girls to the big city and made a small splash of brilliant spangles in what the family snidely described as, "The Theater."

Two of Aunt Sophie's sisters, Lucy and Lydia, were twins. Each married boys they knew from town and produced three children who they neglected and smothered in spurts, depending on whether they were drinking heavily or rediscovering religion, both which they did frequently. The last sister, Herminie, married late, being nearly twenty-seven. For a while it was feared she would be another "poor" spinster like Sophie. But, she married a good man and had one child, the only real criminal the family ever produced. The boy was attracted to what he considered stagnant money in banks, and unable, after stealing it, to resist setting fire to the building, using the President's desk as a base, and wills, mortgages and the like for tinder. He wasn't brought up much in family discussions.

The pride of the family though, for having kids was my Grand-mother Mandy (Amanda) who married at fifteen and in the next twenty-five years gave birth to eighteen children, one of whom was my father. Only fourteen of them survived entry into the family but these fourteen grew from healthy and lusty kids into healthy, lusty and often hell-raising, adults. Naturally enough these children of Mandy's, and the other married sisters and brother, produced even more children. Aunt Sophie was never without resources.

As Mandy's older sister, Sophie's 'career' started naturally enough with the birth of Araminta, Mandy's first child. Mandy was barely sixteen and nervous about the whole affair. Her husband Zed, my Grandfather, ran the local bar. He spent the event in town, his customers helped him celebrate the birth.

Aunt Sophie delivered the child and declared her to be, "Rather ugly but she has nice hands and feet." Despite Mandy's protests she stayed to help with the canning and never returned home.

By late 1918 Mandy had a total of four children and Aunt Sophie had helped birth them all, including number four, my Father, Wilber.

For some reason that no one knew but everyone gave thanks for, Mandy didn't have any children for the next few years. Some cynics said that with the war over Zed didn't need to keep producing dependents, but, whatever the reason, it gave everyone a much needed rest, at least temporarily.

Aunt Sophie stayed until Wilber was walking and then, with no new births on the horizon, she went to Cannon Beach where Willie and Zack were working on the roads. She kept house for them for some months and "worked out" for a couple of years. That was the story the family knew, and the one I'd grown up with. I never suspected, because I was, in essence, more interested in myself than in her 'old days', that there was more to those years than I knew. Incredibly more.

In that time she knew love.

3. I've Never Told Anyone

She told me the story only once, over that Labor Day weekend, with such vividness and determination that I feel compelled to re-tell it, so that we can know the finality of it, and forgive the fragility.

Usually her tales were told as she worked about the house, or on her quilts. This one began that mid-Friday afternoon as we were picking blackberries. It was a beautiful September day, the time of year in Oregon when the seasons hang suspended - no longer summer, not yet fall.

Though she was old, her back was still straight and her face had a rosy, girlish joy as the berries piled up in the pail attached to her low-slung belt. A bee swung a bit too close to her face and she pulled back involuntarily, scratching her hand on the sharp briars.

"Cottonpickin' thunderbolts!" she said, shaking her hand and sucking at the bit of blood that welled up. She laughed easily to herself, then looked over at me. Her rosy cheeks and soft black eyes - she was pretty, as I'd never seen her before. I'd never seen her as pretty, or homely, she was just Aunt Sophie, always there, and always the same.

"Annie," she asked, a question in her tone, "did I ever tell you about David?" I searched the family quickly, no David came to mind. "No, of course I didn't," she went on, "I've never told anyone."

"Who is David?" I prodded as she seemed to sink into reflection. Was this a hint of the senility I was now on the lookout for?

"Aw, David," she said as if the name felt good on her tongue. She tasted it again. "David Andrew Smithers." I could tell that the "Smithers" part didn't taste as well. "Smithers," she said again, her lips wrinkling then smoothing with her smile. "Aw, well, he couldn't help that."

"What's wrong with 'Smithers'," I pressed, anxious lest she dismiss the whole thing before I found out who this David Andrew was that made her smile so.

"It's not artistic enough. David was an artist." Here she broke off to suggest, "How about we sit in the shade for awhile?"

There were still lots of berries on the vines and, Aunt Sophie never stopped until every container available, plus her apron, was full, so I quickly agreed, knowing that this tale was somehow different, important. We settled ourselves on a grassy spot and leaned against the trunk of a large fir.

"Now," I asked lightly, "who is David Andrew Smithers?"

"David was mine."

4. Walking Carefully

You know that Amanda had Zed, and the twins had Jack and Edward, and even Hermie eventually got her Zorba." She wasn't asking me, it was a statement of fact. I nodded. She repeated, "Well, David was mine." She took a deep breath, settling herself more firmly onto the ground. "He was mine, but he belonged to someone else.

The winter that your father was learning to walk, I got a letter from Zack. He and Willie were batching it in a small cabin near Cannon Beach. Zack wanted me to come down and keep house for them. The ocean was beautiful in winter he said and they had a grand view from their window. It would be a big help if I could just add a feminine touch to the place. He meant do all their 'womanly' work for them, of course! But it sounded romantic to me and Mandy had been kinda testy lately. The winter supplies were in and she could handle the kids and Zed by herself now that she was all of 20, so I went.

When I got there it was the middle of November, but warm. The cabin was bigger than I expected, with two small bedrooms. Willie and Zack shared one and I had the other one all to myself. After all the years of sharing a bed with either a sister or one of Mandy's kids, it felt good to have a whole bedroom all to myself, let alone my own bed. It was just a simple cot, with a straw mattress. I wanted to make a quilt for it so Willie made me a frame to work on. While the boys were at work, after I had my chores done, I'd get out my scrap bag, which goes everywhere I do, and cut pieces.

The boys were glad to have me. They were only seventeen and sixteen that first winter and Willie especially missed the motherly nagging - though you'd never have known it to hear them talk! They loved being on their own and making their own pay. They blew half of their wages every Saturday night at the dance hall saloon in Seaside. Before I came they blew almost all of it. After a couple of bad weekends I made them give me half of it before they went to town. They didn't like it but it was the only way I could make sure that we had food on the table and that the rent got paid. I marked three envelopes, one for Willie, one for Zack, and one for myself and put in three dollars a week for each of us in the envelopes.

Zack never really appreciated it, especially the money I kept for myself. Naturally, he made the most work for me. Zack still thinks women were born to serve him, which is why he never got a women to stay with him for long. Our natures were never very sympathetic to each other. I fancied myself a suffragette and resented his attitude towards me.

I have to admit this too, I liked my position as older sister. I made the most of the opportunity to boss Zack around without Mom there to interfere. He fought me, but because he had asked me to come, he had little ground to stand on. Not if he wanted dinner!

Willie was different. He was grateful for everything I did for him. Zack was a terrible cook and housekeeper so Willie was delighted with the clean cabin and my apple pies, thick bean soups and the chowders I learned to make.

The kitchen was mine. Not Mandy's or my mother's. Mine. I filled the windowsills with shells from the things we caught and that we found. There was a mist of sand on the sills from the wind through the cracks around the window frames. The stove worked best for me, the boys could never get it right. And then I would show them how to build the right kind of fire .. it irritated them, which was of course why I did it. That was my most favorite kitchen, even more than David's. The boys were more than glad to have me take over.

The boys taught me how and where to dig for the razor clams on the beach. And how to get the blue-shelled mussels that we steamed and dipped in melted butter. Mmm, so good.

We got the mussels from the rocks and the tide pools at Haystack when the water was just covering them. Most of the time I could just twist them off the rocks, sometimes I had to use a knife to cut them loose. Whenever the tide was right or I was just tired of beans and smoked pork, I'd take my shovel and knife down to the beach and get mussels and all kinds of clams. The smell of salt in the air, the sun shining on my back, or the fog swirling around .. I still miss it.

We went fishing in the surf when it wasn't too rough. We had fish fried, baked, and in soup until we were sick of it and glad to get back to bread and beans. Once in a while we took a little boat and went crabbing. I don't know who it belonged to. It sat up above the beach and we'd just put it back when we were done. Truth to tell, I loved going out over the waves onto the ocean. It was just scary enough to be fun, but I trusted the boys to be able to get us out and back. Didn't do it often 'cause the ocean was pretty rough most of the time. Zack made a crab pot out of some wire and net he got from a fisherman friend. It was a round thing that you throw in the water weighted with some fishing lead. We'd tie some stinky fish to the net and throw it in the water from the boat, come back about an hour or so later and pull it up. One of my jobs was to dip the bucket we brought along into the ocean, leaning over the edge of the boat and scooping it about half full of water. Getting crabs was fun, like a surprise party every time we pulled that thing up. They'd be scooting around in there trying to get out and Zack would just grab 'em and throw 'em in the bucket. I was scared they'd grab me! They'd scritch and scratch around in there until we got 'em home put 'em out of their misery by throwing them in a pot of boiling water. Cooked in the salt water I'd got from the ocean, with a bit of nutmeg, they weren't bad but I never was crazy about them like the boys were. And David.

Willie shot a deer just before Thanksgiving soon after I came, and, what we didn't eat fresh I canned and made into mincemeat with a good amount of vinegar. That boy just loved my mincemeat pies!

Smacked his lips over the big pieces I'd give him.

But he was rough too. Both the boys were rough. That was the way with all the men in our family, I didn't think much about it.

Their manners were terrible. They belched at the table and never excused themselves. Their hands were callused and unclean looking from the rough road work they did. I made them wash for meals. They had to be reminded to comb their hair (except on Saturday nights), and the only clothes they had were work clothes, the red plaid shirts and dark work pants.

On Saturday night, Zack, in particular, had a regular ritual of cleaning up. He washed his hands and face real good, changed his work socks for his nicer, dancing socks. Most of all, he polished his shoes, his special dancing shoes, something the other guys (certainly not Willie), didn't have. He'd get out his black polish and his special rag and after cleaning off the stuff left on his shoes from the week before, he whip those dancing shoes into shape - you know, polish and spit and polish and spit. They were pretty! When he got done he'd put those shoes on and walk different. Careful not to get in any mud. He carried a piece of cloth in his pocket to spiff them up just before he and Willie went into the hall.

There was a dance hall over to Seaside where everybody went. The boys had an old buggy that one of the guys from the road crew got from somebody. They'd all go over in that. I didn't much like the road as it was close to the cliffs in a couple places - rough cut and narrow. They guys all had the same idea of a great time, going to the dance hall with plenty of liquor and dancing with the wild girls they met there. Sometime early in the morning one of the guys from Seaside would dance with one of the girls that belonged to a guy from the road crew and she would laugh too much at his jokes - the fight would be on. It was the same every Saturday night. Willing girls, too much whisky, wild dancing, then the fight. The ride home was a sobering experience with the trees leaning in close and who knows what out there in the dark. At least the horses only drank water so everybody always made it home in one piece.

I know because I would go with them. I liked the dancing, and yes, the drinking. The men all had strong arms and spared no expense on showing a fun-loving gal a good time. They were young and so was I. My hair was down to the middle of my back, and dark, then. Ebony-black David called it. I was, of course, as tall then, (well, taller, I suppose but not much) than I am now. Five feet seven. I was full-hipped (not just broad like now), and high breasted .. and my waist was small so that it narrowed-in nicely. The men like to grab me around the middle and twirl me around, and even David like to run his hands down my sides and, 'Measure the hourglass,' he said.

I was never especially pretty, I was what they called then, handsome. But David said that when I laughed, I was beautiful.

David lived in the house above us. It wasn't a cabin, it was a real house that David and his wife had designed and built themselves. They got wood from all sorts of places, some that washed up on the beach, some lumber that they bought from Seaside, and then David had cut down some trees from up in the woods. The house was much longer than it was wide, being only about thirty feet deep. It faced the ocean and was a two-storied affair with what they called a 'cupola' on top, right in the middle. The cupola looked like a fancy chicken coop to me. It was glass all around, except for the wooden frame. You could open up the window front and back to let the air blow through. David loved to sit up there in the summer and paint. Painting was the way he made his living, and his passion. When he tired of painting he would turn to his telescope and watch the seals over by Ecola Bay.

The second floor of the house was their bedroom. There was also a smaller bedroom, which was meant to be a child's room, but, in their twelve years of marriage, no children had come. They used it mostly for storing David's paintings.

The downstairs was one big, long room. The kitchen was at one end and a big stone fireplace was at the other end. The fireplace also went up into their bedroom, which was upstairs.

There was a big window downstairs, with a long bench in front of it. Painted yellow. With Christmas cactus on it. It was pretty. I remember violets and geraniums in that window, too. All kind of plants new to me. My folks never had much use for plants in the house, things needed to be useful. But everything did well there. Most surprising to me was the bookcase. We didn't have much cause or time for reading at home so almost a whole wall for books was odd to me. Against the back wall, it reached from floor to ceiling. The supports were hand-notched. In bare places were a few knick knacks, but mostly shells. Lots of shells.

In the few feet of space not taken up by the bookcase was a small, paned window looking back over the property into trees. In winter with some of the trees and bushes bare you could see if someone passed by on the road above. Under the window was the sewing machine, beside which was a large humpbacked trunk, used for storing material and Amy's sewing stuff.

Over by the front door was where everybody hung their coats and hats, and all sorts of other things: buckets, clamming shovels, a lantern. I've forgotten what all. David kept saying he was going to build a porch to hide it all proper-like, but he never did.

I didn't meet David until spring came, but I saw him every day. A path led from his house to the beach and it passed within a few feet of our cabin. I didn't notice him for the first two or three days - I was too busy cleaning and cooking, but soon after I had the household setting into a routine I noticed him.

I was standing at the window watching the ocean. It was early, about 6:00 a.m. The morning light was just starting to show. It was stormy as I remember, not like it gets in mid-winter, but I'd lived inland all of my life and never seen any kind of sea storm so I was fascinated. Seagulls were out there flying into the wind, catching updrafts and in general just having a good time. I saw something move out of the corner of my eye, I turned and looked. It was a man walking slowly right by our cabin, walking carefully so as not to slip on the slick grass. Once in a while he would look down to check his footing, but mostly he walked with his head high. He was looking all around feeling the wind and smelling the air, but when he walked past my window he looked away, so he wouldn't be staring in our place, you know. He was very polite, David was.

5. Who Is That Fellow?

I couldn't see his face because he was going away from me but I looked him over careful. I was already 22 years old, remember, and I'll admit it, every man was a possibility. He wasn't tall, five feet, about eight and a half inches and even dressed like he was I could tell he didn't have much meat on him.

He had on a heavy oilskin coat like fishermen wear, and high rubber boots. The hood of his coat was thrown back but he had on an old, yellow souwester protecting his neck and ears from the wind. His pants were black, and lumpy, like he had another pair under them. His hands were stuffed in his pockets most of the time, 'cept when he took them out to steady himself. He looked like a fisherman but he didn't have a pole, so I wondered what he was doing.

I watched him go down the path, slow and careful, then he disappeared 'round the bend in the trail. I went to the front window and kept watching. Pretty soon I saw him walk out on the beach, right toward the waves. I thought for a minute that maybe he was crazy, you know, going to walk right out there and drown himself or something, but then I thought, he's too dressed up for that, unless he wants to die warm. But he just walked in the water at the edge for a long way down the beach 'till I got bored watching him. I got the broom and started sweeping sand from the floor to out the door.

The sand! Always sand on the floor! Nearly drove me mad crunching underfoot and clinging to my shoes and hiding between my toes so that I always had to wash my feet before climbing into bed at night.

About an lour later I saw him coming back up the path. I stood at the window and watched him come. I guess I was kinda bold but how else was I going to see his face if I didn't look at him? He was holding some shells, sand dollars I think, in one hand, and his poor hands looked cold and raw, and red. I didn't think he saw me, so I continued to stare at him.

I put my hand up to smooth my hair and I guess the motion caught his eye 'cause suddenly he looked up, straight at me. And he grinned.

He was no more than four feet away from me and that big grin just about turned my heart over. I didn't mind staring at him, but I didn't expect him to be bold right back!

His eyes were blue - bright blue topped by wild, bushy red eyebrows, and his teeth were very white. He had a red mustache that curled on the ends, but otherwise he was clean shaven. His face was raw from the wind, especially his cheekbones. His face all over was almost too sweet, but the sharp cheekbones and mustache gave him a dashing appearance. I still don't know whether it was the smile or his eyes that did me in.

I was so startled when he grinned at me that I was almost scared, but I couldn't help myself, I smiled right back. He nodded, then was gone past the cabin, up the path back to his strange house.

From then on I watched him nearly every day. He was as regular as the clock. Down the path at 6:00, an hour on the beach, then back past the cabin about 7:00. And always, unless I was out clamming, or something, I stood there and watched him go by. And always he looked in at me and smiled that grin. I was like a fascinated thing. I could no more keep away from that window than I could stop breathing.

I lived that winter on David's smiles. I thought of him during the day as I worked and I dreamed of him at night when I slept. I would be embarrassed to tell you about those dreams! When I got up at 4:00 in the morning the thought that I would soon see him warmed me as I made the fire in the cookstove. He sometimes walked past near dusk but I usually ignored him then because the boys were there.

The boys didn't suspect a thing. On Saturday nights I went to the dances with them and had a good enough time, but I was always hoping he'd be there. He never was of course, he was at home with his wife.

I didn't know he had a wife. I'd blocked the possibility right out of my mind. David had no wife in my dreams, except maybe me. I didn't know until one day, in late winter, when David walked past one evening when I was staring out the window watching some gulls argue over something on the beach. It would have been unnatural to have ignored the fact that a man was walking right by the window so I casually asked the boys, "Do you guys know who that fellow is out there?"

Zack looked up and snorted, "Sure, that's crazy Smithers."

"Crazy Smithers?" I asked, my heart dropping. But I tried to sound casual, like it was just an ordinary conversation and I didn't care much.

"Yeah," said Willie. "Some of the guys call him that 'cause he's a painter. But I don't think he's crazy."

"A painter?"

"Yeah, of pictures," he looked at me, making a square with his hands like a frame. My relief was confused. I wasn't sure a painter was a 'real man'. You understand, Annie?

"Well, if he's not crazy he's probably .. unnatural .. which is just about the same thing." I was feeling rather queasy.

"Naw, Zack, he's nothing ... he's just different! He uses his hands to make a living just like we do, 'cept he paints with his. I saw him down to the beach a couple a times last summer, painting. He was painting birds and people poking around Haystack Rock and it looked real real, you know, almost like a photograph."

"Yeah?" questioned Zack, giving Willie a funny look. "That proves it, only weird people mess around drawing pictures when they should be working."

"No, you're wrong, Zack. I know it."

"Yeah? How?"

"He had his wife with him," Willie answered flatly. My heart felt like a rock. I didn't know whether to be crushed, or relieved.

"Yeah?" asked Zack. Women always interested him. "Is she a painter, too? What's she look like?"

"No, I don't think so. She was just lying on a blanket in the sun. She's kinda frail looking. Short, blondish hair and big brown eyes. Little woman. There was something about her didn't seem too strong. She was sorta pale, like she didn't get out much. But she was real nice. Friendly. Sweet-like."

"Humph," Zack grunted. You could tell he was thinking it over. "Still, I wouldn't let the guys see you hanging around Smithers. They might get wrong thoughts."

Willie just let the subject drop but his mouth had the set look it got when he'd made up his mind he was going to do what he dang well pleased. But what Zack said must of stayed with him because next summer he avoided going down to the beach when he knew David was there. He didn't speak to David again until the day he caught us.

6. The Beach in Winter

I wasn't idle that winter, though I certainly didn't keep a spotless house. That winter was not a problem of too little to do, but too much. Other than clammin' and fishing there was plenty of housework. We got water from a rain barrel at the side of the cabin, plus what the boys got from a well in town. They had a crude washing setup at the side of the cabin with a couple tin tubs that I washed and rinsed in. They'd put a rough roof over that spot, with a few lines strung across. I had a couple lines in the house that I hung clothes on when it was wet outside.

After the work was done, the cabin cleaned and bread set to rise, I'd get to work on my quilts. One for Zack, one for Willie, and finally, one for myself. Zack and Willie's were traditional: a plain square for Zack, 'cause he didn't like anything, "too fancy," and a star quilt for Willie. His was many colored, with even some flower pieces from old dresses. I wouldn't dare use flowers on Zack's! He'd a burned it up!

Mine was different, big enough for a double bed, 'cause I still had hopes! But sort of modernistic I guess you would call it now. I wanted to capture the ocean, but I couldn't get it right. I was trying to copy the seashore with a sandy gray, the sun with a bright yellow circle, and the different blues of the sky and the sea with broad bands of varied and pale violets, but it was defeating me. The sky and the water looked different depending on the weather. I particularly wanted to capture the sea as I'd seen it the first days after I arrived. The contrast in the weather, for one day had been brilliantly appealing, sunny and warm, and the next was foggy cold and windy .. stunned me into a love for the sea that I've never lost, though I came to dread the many endless days of thick fog through the next bitter, lonely winter.

The boys had picked me up in the late afternoon from the train in Seaside so that by the time we arrived at the cabin I'd seen only little glimpses of the ocean from the road above. The sun was low in the sky when I got my first full view of the shore. We were carting my belongings down the path to the cabin when I stopped and looked at the ocean. In front of me was all blue and green water, moving and foamy, stretching 'till it met the faraway sky which was a different blue, with clouds reflecting up the blues of water and sky. I just threw my stuff on the floor and right then and there challenged Willie and Zack to a race to the waves. They won - they were stronger and running through dry sand is hard!

But once I got on the wet, firm part I sprinted barefoot for the shallow water and ran splashing by them towards the waves. The water rolled in to greet me, all foamy, but I turned and ran down through the surf towards the big rock that was just sitting there. It looked so close, but the distance was deceptive. Before long I was out of breath and little closer. The boys caught up with me and we strolled through the shallow water, splashing it into a fine spray with my toes. It was cold on my toes! Not like river water at home in the summer. When the sun started to set on the horizon, my brothers turned me around to walk up to a drier spot to sit on the sand and watch the sunset.

"Just look, Sophie!" exclaimed Willie, happy to have someone from home to show this off to, "Ain't it beautiful?"

The sun was a round, red blaze sinking into dazzling blue water, casting up a pink, and pale blue, sky before, above, and all around us.

"Ummm, Ummmm." was all I could say. So quickly, before I could absorb the glory, it was over. The sun flattened out like a stepped-on rubber ball, then slipped into the ocean.

"Couldn't you almost hear it sizzle?" whispered Zack as we stood silently in the twilight. He surprised me. Zack was not known for his sensitive nature. I couldn't resist the urge to tease him a bit.

"Why, Zack, I think you've got a poet's soul! Willie! Did you hear what he said?"

"Ah-h-h, Soph," Willie kidded, using his childhood name for me, "leave the poor guy alone. A night like this would turn anyone's head, even a tough heart like Zack!" Zack was glaring at both of us, saying nothing.

Poor Zack, he so seldom opened up like that, and we crushed him. As the oldest boy no one ever let him forget that he had to see things clearly, with no romantic haze.We could be as silly as we wanted he must maintain a toughness, be a 'real man'. I hadn't learned yet that a real man could be both tough, and tender.

We strolled home, getting to the cabin just as dark set in.

I went to bed early, bone tired from the ride and the play on the beach. Hours later I woke up. There were no windows in my room and it was dark and stuffy. I laid for a few minutes with the blankets thrown back shaking the warm nightclothes away from my body, trying to whip up a cool breeze. The longer I laid there the heavier the air seemed. I could hear the boys in the next room, one of them snoring loudly, fairly shaking the front room window, the other breathing heavy in the close room. At first it was funny listening to them competing with the noisy ocean but I couldn't go back to sleep. They jangled my nerves until I finally got up and found my old robe in the dark. I felt my way through the curtain into the lighter front room.

Moonlight was forcing it's way through the dirty window. The air was fresher in the larger room, but not much. Outside had to be better, and away from the snoring!

The night was warm and unusually dry. Willie had said it hadn't rained for days. The grass was sandy and dry under my bare feet. Away from the protection of the cabin a fresh wind brushed my face and blew my hair against my neck.

Trees and beach alike were patterned in moon shadows bouncing off some dark clouds above. The moon was full and white. It lit the way easily. I walked to the lip of the little hill overlooking the beach, sat down carefully and gave myself up to the warm beauty of the night.

I was admiring the silhouette of Haystack and watching the waves breaking on the low tide when I noticed something I'd not seen in the daytime, white fire on the waves! As they broke and ran down the beach the foam shimmered. I held my breath as diamonds of fire sparkled on the waves.

On my far right I could see a faint twinkle of light from the ocean. At first I thought it was coming from a ship, then I realized it was from a rock out in the ocean. A lighthouse sitting on a rock in the sea, its' light blinking in a steady rhythm.

I sat for a while soaking up the romantic atmosphere, feeling lonelier by the minute. It was a night made for love. A full moon, tide out, fresh warm air, running waves of fire shimmering on the dark sea with only the single man-made light sparkling in the dark. I longed for a strong arm to pull me close, a bristly cheek to brush against my neck, tender hands and lips to share this moonlit night with. But try as I did, I couldn't conjure up a vision of anyone special I wanted with me. It was frustrating.

Opening my eyes I took in the scene around me once more, sighed, and let my practical nature take over. It was long after midnight, I should be in bed. I'd left the cabin door open, the fresh air had calmed the boys' dreams so that the cabin was peacefully quiet and cool. Sleep came easily.

Waking early the next morning I dressed quickly, went to the front room window and saw water, a wide, white beach of waves running far down both ways from the window. And rocks, huge rocks, including the one with the lighthouse on it, scattered all up and down the coast just a little ways out from the surf, like dark guardians of the ocean. We had a grand view from that cabin.

I rushed through breakfast with the boys, packed their lunch buckets, waved them off to work and threw a light jacket and a scarf on and went out to a wonderful, sunny morning.

The tide was partially out. As soon as I got down the bank I took off my shoes and left them there with my socks stuffed in. Who was going to steal them? Following the same route as the day before I was determined to get to the big rock. It didn't seem as far away as before, probably because I was rested. The early morning beach was strewn with what I soon learned were sand dollars, a round, white shell about three inches across with an interesting design of five finger- like markings spread from a base like thick sunrays. I put them in my pockets, plus lots of small, orange fan-shaped shells, and some other kinds 'till my jacket pockets were full. I couldn't swing my arms for fear I'd crack the shells.

The ocean looked like a big turquoise cake with creamy white frosting spilling over the edge. The sky was flat with no color, clear, bright, no clouds whatsoever. From a distance Haystack Rock shimmered green in the sun, closer up I saw it was a thick, dark green moss and a tough grass that grew out of cracks in the side of the rock. It was the base of the rock that intrigued me most. I'd never seen a tide pool, or so many seagulls, or the little sandpipers. They were so cute. I miss 'em. They hopped and pecked at the blue mussels and ivory barnacles that covered the rocks of the tide pools.

Seagulls squawked at me, and each other, and at the sandpipers, making a big show of protecting their rocks, but flapping away when I got too close. They'd settle down again on the rocks just a little further away, screaming at me. I laughed but the sandpipers took them seriously, skittering away across the sand then coming back when the gulls moved away. The little birds moved in a group but the gulls were separate, each bird for himself.

Some rocks close up beside Haystack, smaller but still big, reminded me of giant thumbs pointing towards the sky, a 'thumbs up' position that further cheered me to the delights of the morning. I spent a couple of hours just looking at the tide pools that had little bitty crabs and swimmy things that dashed away when I tried to touch them. And anemones, the squishy, purple, soft things that squeezed shut when I put my fingers on their sticky edges. The farm never had anything like this! I was like a kid, wondering how everything worked and why the barnacles were so rough and hard while other things acted like animals when I touched them. I didn't know the names of things at first, of course, but the guys all told me the details over the time I was there. Men love to tell you everything they know.

But the sun was blinding white and despite the light breeze, the sleep I'd missed the night before caught up with me. I needed to go home before I fell asleep on the beach. The walk back was slow because I kept stooping to pick up gray and black feathers and more shells and to look at the glass-like globs that were all over the beach. They juggled when I poked them with a black feather; I was afraid to touch anything that looked like it might be alive. Later the boys laughed at me being afraid of dead jellyfish.

By the time we went to bed that night the wind was really blowing through the trees, but it was hot and sleepless again. After getting the boys off to work in the morning I went back to bed and didn't get down to the beach until late morning. The tide was high, way in, and the wind was tearing down the beach. Even with one of Zack's heavy jackets on, the long walk towards Elk Creek up the other way, away from Haystack towards where the lighthouse light had shown, was cold, windy, and miserable. Shells were scarce and the wind threw sand in my face –it stung– so I had to keep my head down. I finally got to the creek, noted it running fresh into the ocean, and happily turned to go home. The wind pushed me back to the warm cabin. I added wood to the stove and from my snug harbor watched the gulls flying into the wind and ocean tumbling onto the sand. I got out my quilt bag and played with cloth, fingering the pieces I had and comparing them with what I saw out the window.

To transfer all the moods and shades of the sea to simple cloth seemed about impossible. How to show the feeling of differences in the fogs? Dark, gray sky and water through a light fog was different from when the fog rolled in so thick that everything was gone, nothing but gray, coldness everywhere. I hated the thick fog, it closed me in. I felt trapped, shut off from the world. But the light fog, it's beautiful swirling in and around the trees, a thick layer of gray lace tangling lightly with the branches. Lovely too, because it would soon be gone, bringing, at least light, and sometimes, the precious sun.

There was hope in the light, despair in the thickness. I knew I'd have to make the back of my quilt a solid gray to represent the fog. "The Beach in Winter" I called it.

But the frontpiece was giving me fits. Until near spring when I remembered what Willie had said about David painting Haystack Rock. That was it! I'd put Haystack in the middle on a background of bright blue. The rock would be reddish brown, like it is sometimes when the evening sunset turns the sky red. Surrounding the big square would be yellow suns, embroidered all the way 'round. The border would be a pale blue quilted to look like waves.

I started with the Rock, as it was the central, most important piece, drawing its' shape on a pad I had left from school and kept in my quilt bag. The Rock was in clear view from the front window, except when hidden by fog. I spent hours trying to copy it. I couldn't get it. The harder I tried the worse it looked. I'd make it too big for anything else to be around it. I couldn't get how it looked with the whole of the sea and sky surrounding it. I spent many hours by the window sketching it in different weathers. Finally I put it away and went back to work on the boy's quilts.

7. What Are You Doing Here...?

Along about the end of March the weather started clearing. It was still rainy and foggy most of the time, but the long winter was finally coming to an end.

After I learned that David was married, I wasn't at the window so often. For the first three days or so I hid in my bedroom when I saw him leave the beach below, and only came out when I was sure he'd had time to pass. But finally I could stand it no longer, I missed his smile too much. If my romantic dreams couldn't come true I could at least be friendly. The poor man, I thought, stuck in the house with a sick wife, probably a whiney invalid. Perhaps our daily exchange was as important to his life as it was to mine - in a different way of course. By that time, David had assumed such saintly proportions that I couldn't conceive of him being unfaithful to his wife, however much a trial she was to him.

On the fourth day, I had gone into my bedroom as usual, but after a few minutes I spread the curtain cautiously and looked across the room out the window. David had just come in view and he was looking directly at the cabin. His face had a searching, troubled look and his shoulders were slumped.

I couldn't bear to see him like that. I came out and walked over to the window.

As soon as I appeared his whole appearance changed. His shoulders went back, his step was lighter and his face lit up in a big smile.

I was exhilarated and terrified. His hold on me was total, and I knew it. And we'd never even spoken a word. As he passed he stopped and said, "I missed you." Then he went on. I couldn't hear the words but I knew what he had said.

The rest of the day was a haze. I tried to sew, and couldn't. His words kept repeating in my brain, "I missed you I missed you I missed you." I had imaginary conversations with him where I went out the door and took his hands in mine and looking deep into his eyes said, 'I missed you, too.'

'Come away with me,' he pleaded.

'But your wife?'

'What wife? I have no wife.'

'But, the woman on the beach?'

'Oh, that was my sister who was ill and here for the sea air, but she is gone now so come and live with me in my beautiful house!'

'Gladly,' I answered.

Thus I easily dismissed the wife. She didn't exist for David and me. Still I had sense enough to try to cool my behavior. I seldom stood at the window anymore. When he came by, I would be busy sweeping or kneading bread, or at the stove. He would get a nod or a slight wave but I kept my face busy, paying attention to the work I was doing. He must not know how completely he had me, how I lived each day to see him, a man I didn't even know.

Round about the end of March, first of April, I started working outside on the garden. I would wait till David was home again and then go out. I cleared a large area of ground, pulling out ferns and salal, and roots. You wouldn't believe the roots! That ground had never been dug. Lucky it was so sandy. Still it was a hard job. It took a couple more days than I thought it would to get it done, and the main reason I got it done even then was because Willie and Zack each put in some time before dinner a couple evenings. They pounded those roots and chopped 'em till the whole patch was a fine mash. The sweat was just 'a flying! They turned it all over for me. By the end of April I had the garden put to some vegetables plus some dirt spaded up by the front door and around the cabin for flowers. It was inevitable that working near the path so often I would meet David.

You might wonder at him never knocking on my door and introducing himself, as a neighbor might, or why he didn't just 'chance by' when I was working on the garden. I, well ... I don't think he was any more anxious to meet the real me than I was him. Dreams were a lot easier to deal with than reality, and too, David thought I was the wife of one of the boys.

On the first day of May I got up early. Spring was in the air and the morning was warm. I had a couple of rose bushes I'd bought the week before at the general store in town, red climbers, and I knew when I got up that this was the day to plant them.

David went by, at 6:00 as usual. I had my morning coffee and then, thinking I had plenty of time, went to the woodshed for the roses and spade. When I came back around to the front David was coming up the path.

There was nothing to do but to act like it was a normal thing to see him there. To bolt into the house would have looked foolish. Standing there with the spade in one hand and a rosebush in the other I said, "Morning!"

He stopped, startled. He'd been looking at the tiny yellow flowers by the path and hadn't seen me. At my voice he looked up, then came straight towards me, that big grin spreading on his face, his hand outstretched.

"Why, good morning to you!" His voice was big for such a small man, and didn't sound in the least 'unmanly'. His hand was still outstretched. I leaned the shovel against the cabin and put my hand into his. I shook his hand as natural as anything. I'd never shaken a man's hand before in my life! You young folks do it now but it wasn't something girls did then. It was a pleasant experience! His hands were small with short, narrow fingers, not at all the long artistic hands I'd expected.

I think I was shocked when his hand gripped mine, fearing for a second that he would actually say 'come away with me', but of course he didn't. I was shy face-to-face with him so suddenly. He was almost a stranger. But he didn't act like one. He let go of my hand, and just as natural as if he were continuing a conversation we'd started a while ago, asked, "Planting the roses?"

I came out of my stupor enough to answer, "Why, yes," while my thoughts ran around searching for something smart to say. Nothing came.

"Right here by the door I hope. That's the best place." I nodded dumbly, he went on, "Well, let's get at it." He just lifted that shovel right out of my hand and started digging in the loosened dirt, covering my shyness with talk.

"My mother had roses, a whole arbor of them to the side of the house. I used to play out there under the roses, when I was just a little boy. It was real cool there ... I love roses, don't you?" Before I could answer he laughed, "Dumb question. Of course you do!"

My mind was moving again but I guess I was not in complete control for I blurted out, "What are you doing here?" It sounded more like an accusation than a question. I immediately wished I'd kept my mouth shut but I've always been that way, "Mouth ahead of brain," my daddy used to say.

David stopped his digging, and looked directly at me. I tried to avoid his eyes. "No, look at me." I did, but it was uncomfortable even through the pleasure of looking so straight on at him.

"We," he stopped. "What's your name?" I stumbled it out.

"Sophie," he repeated, making it sound special. "I'm David." I stood still, looking into his eyes, a fascinated thing like the hens would get when the boys petted them on their throats. "Well, Sophie, I'm here because I came back up to get my paints. It's a natural day for painting, as it is for planting roses. But, I knew perfectly well that you would be here, maybe not today, but sometime. We couldn't go on forever seeing each other and never meeting, now could we?"

"Well .. I never really thought about it," I mumbled the lie. This mumbling around was awful. He was going to think I was a complete idiot. Shrugging my shoulders in what I hoped was a casual manner I spoke up more firmly. "No, I guess not. After all," I said lightly, "we're neighbors."

"No Sophie, we're more than neighbors. And you know it. I know it, don't you?"

I struggled against answering but his eyes demanded an answer. An honest answer, and for the life of me I couldn't lie to him. "Yes," then, angry at his forcefulness, I found my tongue. "If we're not just neighbors, what do you think we are?" I didn't want him examining what I thought we were!

"Friends," he answered. The dark blue eyes relaxed their grip on me and became sunny again.

"Friends, Sophie, and Lord knows that's as rare, as, well, as rare as having an ebony-haired beauty greet me every day with a beautiful smile!"

'Ebony-haired beauty'! Me? I'd never had a man speak so fancy to me before. Once a fellow at a dance who'd had too much to drink told me I was, "a great looking dame," and men had certainly said fresh things to me when making passes, but most men had to have something to drink before they could get brave enough to even approach me. Mandy said I scared them off, but I don't know why. And then, during the war they were either gone or when they came back they seemed gripped by a frenzy to get married, an idea that always chilled me. The life of my mother, or my sister, was not what I wanted. Sometimes I scared myself. I was already 22 and all I knew was that I didn't want to lose my freedom. But it was all confused with the feelings that at times nearly overcame me. At least David seemed safe.

He turned to the roses. He was relaxed, and with a silent sigh of relief, I relaxed too. Together we planted the roses. Maybe they're still there. They took hold right away and by the end of September were blooming so much that David cut some to take to his wife.

8. If You Want Me...

After that I was usually outside when he passed. As the summer took hold, David lost the routine of winter. Often he stopped to pass the time of day with me. Those were times of complete happiness for me. I began to take lots of walks on the beach, collecting the shells thrown up or left behind by the waves. It became an obsession to see what new things were there. I found and kept so many that I felt guilty being so greedy. I wrote Mandy to tell the kids that I was collecting shells for them. It sounded so good I believed it myself.

More often than not as I walked farther and farther I 'happened' upon David. His favorite place was near a stump far up the beach. From that angle, early in the morning, the sunshine played on the Rock so that parts were in shadow.

He didn't just paint the Rock, he painted everything: the sea at storm, the seals, the gulls, many different places along the shore. He got tangled up in the colors, too, like me and my quilt. It was his fascination with the different shades of sand, and the different light - morning light and afternoon light, cloud light and sun light - shadows, rain drops and the bird footprints that added the depth to my quilt that it finally had. I've never looked at sand the same since.

And people. Sometimes he went to town or back in the hills to the farms. David knew most of the people who lived up in 'the mountains'. The Hosmer family lived up one of those dirt roads. About once a week David visited them, liking to have lunch with them but more, he loved seeing the children as they were, natural, so he could paint them later. He didn't want them posed, he watched them as they worked around the farm and did quick sketches that he finished in the winter. There was the Hosmer dad, and mother, and five kids. Three boys and two girls. Funny I should think of that now.

My favorite painting of his - oh, the mother's mother lived with them too, - was of one of the girls picking raspberries in their little patch with the grandma. The little girl was about six and had a little pail with a wire handle on it like her grandma's. Her face, in the picture, had just a little raspberry juice on her lips, and the most self-satisfied smile. Just a comfortable thing she was there, in the patch with her grandma. All to herself. The grandma had white hair that was kinda twirly 'round her head. She wore a flowered dress, and boots, and her berry pail hooked onto the old leather belt she had around her waist. She's looking into the bush and reaching through to get a berry from the middle.

I always loved that picture. It was just inside their front door and sometimes I'd look at it and I'd be the grandma, and sometimes I'd be the little girl. It was cool in the bush and hot on our heads. David was good at faces, though he didn't think so.

I was down by the water one day looking for more sand dollars to use as models for my quilt. But, I was picking up everything else that wasn't broke when I saw David waving at me to come over. My apron was full of the shells so I walked rather that ran over to him, like I wanted to. The sand underfoot was white and dry, it squeaked as I crossed it. Seagulls and crows were flying up and down the beach, looking to be more in play than serious hunting for food. When I got to David he untied my apron so I could put the shells down. His face was a sight! His nose was sunburned and peeling. His reddish hair was windblown and sticking up every which way. To me he was the prettiest thing on the beach.

Something had him excited. After taking off my apron he lifted me up on a stump and with his arm around my waist to steady me, he pointed out to sea. I was more aware of his closeness and his hand at my waist than of where he was pointing but as I looked I saw what he was so excited about.

There were three whales playing in the ocean, big, long gray things. The calm sea allowed us see them more clearly than was usual plus they were closer than the ones I was used to seeing from my window.

"I think those are called gray whales," David said, "Gosh, aren't they grand?" They were spouting and diving and looked to be having fun. It made us both giggly. Maybe being so close together had something to do with it, too. He had to hold me tight to keep me from falling, and finally I had to get off the stump before I fell off it.

We sat down in the warm sand and, as we talked he played with it, piling it into mounds, then smoothing them flat. Dribbling handfuls of sand he made designs while asking me about the shells I'd gathered.

"You have so many, going into business or something?" Did he think I was greedy, or silly? I explained about my nieces and nephews, and off-handedly told him about the quilt. He was interested.

"But, David, the center is to be a piece-over of Haystack Rock, and I've tried, and tried, and I can't copy it."

"Sophie, would you mind...?" he hesitated but his face was bright with an idea, plus the sunburn. "One artist shouldn't interfere with another..."

An artist! Me? I would have laughed but he was so serious I just smiled. "But we can help one another. What if I drew it for you?"

I didn't expect his help. "Oh David, you shouldn't waste your time."

His blue eyes were earnest, "I'd like very much to do it."

"Ok." I gave in. "If you insist. I'd really like some help," I admitted. And to you I'll admit that I wanted more than just his help. I wanted the drawing, yes, but because he would be thinking of me while he did it. To know that David was thinking just of me and doing something just for me was a pleasure I wanted very much.

Plus I was flattered. The family always took my quilts for granted, or teased me about my eternal, infernal, 'stitching,' and complained about the little pieces that seemed to float into every nook and cranny of the house. And here David was calling me an artist!

He changed the subject. "So, Sophie, you make quilts, and plant roses. I'm learning more about you every day. Tell me, which of the brothers is your husband, and how long will you be here?"

Me, married to one of my brothers? The idea was so ridiculous and too, my nerves were just stretched thin .. I hooted and laughed till I got a stitch in my side, thinking first of one and then the other as a husband to me.

"What's so funny?" he kept asking. I finally got control of myself and told him our family arrangement. That pleased him.

"I wondered .. I'm glad. The older one seems so gruff and unlike you that I didn't like to think of you married to him. I see him sometimes outside when I pass by in the evening, and he's barely civil. I don't think he approves of me." His eyes twinkled. "And the younger one, he stopped and talked to me on the beach, last year, and seems to like my painting .. but he's too young, too immature .. so," he shrugged, "I wondered."

While he was discussing my brothers as husbands, my mind was on his wife. I didn't want him to speak of her, but maybe I'd made the same mistake he had.

"But you, David, you're married, aren't you?" I hoped he'd laugh too and tell me she was his sister, or his housekeeper, anything but his wife.

"Of course I'm married." He didn't notice my disappointment. I swallowed it and kept smiling brightly at him, while I murmured, "How nice," or something polite, and he went on.

"Amy and I've known each other all our lives. It seems we've always been married. I guess it's been about twelve years now."

"But where is she?" I insisted. "I never see her." I wasn't happy with his tone in speaking of her. He didn't sound at all like a miserable husband.

"You haven't seen Amy because she seldom comes to the beach. She used to come often when we first moved here, about seven years ago, but now she's satisfied to stay at home, reading and taking care.

She writes. When she's not off selling my paintings for me, that is. That's where she is right now, in Salem. She left a week ago. I have a dealer there who sells for me. She delivers a few to him but she has a regular route she follows all around the state, visiting small galleries, and shops, and people she knows who are particularly interested in what I have to sell. She loves to travel! And she really has a knack for selling, which is good, because I hate it. Getting out, seeing all her old friends and meeting new people, it's good for her. Sometimes," he said quietly, "she's gone all summer."

"Then she's not .. sickly?" I wasn't overjoyed at the idea of such a healthy, self-reliant woman.

"Sickly? No. Whatever gave you that idea?"

"Well, Zack saw her last summer here on the beach .." It embarrassed me to admit I'd been talking about him.

The sun went out of his face. "Oh, that. Yes, last summer she wasn't well. For a while." It seemed difficult for him and I wished I hadn't pried.

"We lost our baby." His face tightened. I tried to stop him.

"You don't need to tell me."

He took a long breath.

"Amy was about three months along and we were very happy. We'd waited so long, and had just about accepted that we wouldn't have children when she realized she was carrying a child. She was very careful ... but I guess it wasn't meant to be. Losing the baby was very hard on her. More on her thinking than on her body."

He sat quietly for a while playing with the sand. Gulls screeched from down by the water, fighting over a bit of something washed up in the tide. I couldn't think of what to say. Then he squashed the tower he'd built, "But, it's all right now. We still have time! I'm 35 and she only 33. So! On to a more cheerful subject! How big should my drawing be?"

I was glad to talk of anything else. The last thing I wanted to hear was how happy he and Amy were. I preferred to forget her. As for the quilt I wasn't sure what size the middle piece should be, so he said he'd draw up several sizes and I could choose which one I liked best.

As I got up to leave he put his hand on my shoulder. "I often see you walking on the beach. Please stop by and talk to me again."

"But I don't want to bother you."

"Sophie! I love to talk with you. Your laugh makes me glad." I smiled at that. "And sometimes I just get lonely here by myself. Promise me you'll come again."

"If you want me...."

"I do."

For the next week I saw him on the beach every day, and armed with the invitation always found my way over to him. I limited my time with him and hated leaving, but I was skittish, afraid that if I stayed too long he would know what a dummy I was, or at least what a dummy I thought I was.

For up 'till then no one had ever talked to me, with me, or maybe even more important, listened to me! He wanted to know what I thought! What I thought about books he'd read, whether I ever went out and just looked at the stars at night? Did I believe in God? What was my family like? What did I think happened after a person dies? Did I think there would ever be another war?

Funny things: had I ever seen a ghost, and did I think people had more than one life? If I could travel, where would I go, and why? Did I want to get married and have children? What did I want to do with my life?

I wasn't used to so many questions, and certainly none about most of the things he thought about. I'd take the questions home with me, the strange and new ideas and thoughts spinning in my head, and work out my answers while I sewed and cleaned, or walked on the beach.

Next day I'd go back full of answers and questions of my own and we'd be off again, talking and laughing a mile a minute, until I pulled myself away, frightened by the pull he had upon me. David would always touch me somehow, lightly across my shoulders, fussing about to make sure I was settled comfortably on the sand, taking my hands to help me up when I was leaving. And once he insisted on helping me brush the sand from my skirt when I stood up, causing such a feeling in me that I ran away.

The feelings he raised in me! I was sucked into him, completely absorbed in him, but, oddly, I also felt separate, unique. With him I felt at peace. Alone, or away from him I was confused.

He's married, I kept reminding myself, but the pull just kept getting stronger. Every day I would tell myself, today I'm not going down there, I'll stay at home. But then, he would pass by in the morning and wave, and I'd decide, well, just for a little while this afternoon if I haven't got anything else to do. And the day would go on forever, until I left the cabin, and went to him.

Every day I used the excuse of the drawings to go talk to him. "Are they done yet?" I'd ask and for a couple weeks I waited wondering if he was really working on them or just a talker .. you know how lots of men are .. and every day he'd say, "Just a little bit more, almost done," until it got to be almost a joke for me to tease him and him to pretend that he was working on a masterpiece and I needed to wait for the, "magic of the muse," whatever that meant.

The day it happened ... one day, about a couple of weeks later, after the boys had left for work, I was rummaging through my scrap bag when I heard what I knew was his knock on the door, one of those what they used to call shave-and-a-haircut..two-bits knock. I jerked and scraps fell on the floor. I tidied my hair quickly in the small mirror in my bedroom and tried to appear casual when I opened the door.

He'd never come into the cabin before, he took some time to look around. I let him wander and started coffee, just to have something to do besides stare at him. The fire in the stove was low, it didn't take much but a couple pieces of wood to get it up enough to cook the coffee. He offered to help but I brushed off his offer, I needed to do something with my hands!

My clearest memory of him is the way he looked that day. He

was wearing a blue shirt that set off his eyes and tan prettily. His hair seemed more red, but as usual, it was wild on his head. If I hadn't grabbed the coffeepot I'd have reached for his hair. I always wanted to touch it, pat it, pull my fingers through it.

He walked around the room, then stopped in front of the window. "I like your view." He smacked his lips like he was disappointed. "I tried to get this cabin. This land." I watched him taking in the view, until he turned his head quickly, the sunlight flashing off his hair. His eyes caught mine.

"Oh, really?" I said, just to keep him talking. I didn't care what he was saying. My hands moved to the stove so I could open it and stir the wood about, reaching to the box for another small piece to shove in.

"Un huh," he said, "but Mrs. Hope," our landlady, "said she'd rather rent it out and have some income than sell it and probably waste the money. The land our house is on was hers, too, but she wasn't making anything on it so, she was glad to get rid of it."

He'd come to the shelf Zack had put up for me. I'd put my shells on it, and other doo-dads, just stuff I'd found. Now they took on a glow as he admired and fingered the trinkets with his easy hands. He had his back to me when he asked, "How's the quilt coming along?" and whirled around to pull some sheets of paper out of his back pocket.

The drawings! In the excitement .. I'd forgotten them.

"Oh, David! Let me see!" I took the papers to the window and looked at each one, comparing them to the original, The Rock. They all seemed perfect to me. Then I remembered the scraps in my bag. Were any of them large enough? The reddish-brown from my good dress maybe? Leaving the papers on the windowsill and without even thinking of David, I went to my closet in my bedroom. I had the dress on the bed when David's hand touched me on the shoulder. "I guess you like them? Do I get a thank you?"

I whirled around and straightened up so quickly .. I was face to face with him.

"What?" he asked, "I am sorry! I didn't mean to startle you." He didn't step back.

His breath was warm on my face. His hand reached up to my hair, smoothed down to stroke my face. My hands went to his hair. I was rigid, but my whole body felt alive, pushing towards him. In a last second questioning of myself I pulled back, but he looked at me and pulled me to him, easy.

"Relax," he whispered, "I won't hurt you." His kiss was like velvet, soft and warm, but strong, too. I had the strangest feeling, like I was melting into him. He unbuttoned my dress while I kissed his face and felt the barest stubble of whiskers on my lips. I opened his shirt while his hands moved over my body.

By the time we were down to nothing I didn't want to stop him, or myself. He kept whispering, "So beautiful, so beautiful," as we lay together on my small bed, the brown dress among the heap of clothing on the floor.

I don't know how it was for you, Annie, your first time - I'd heard that a virgin is supposed to feel pain, but I didn't feel any. Only joy, and, afterwards, contented and wrung out. No remorse. That David loved me as completely as I loved him I never had a doubt.

As we lay easy against each other I was at total peace but I felt a tremor startle him. "Oh, Sophie, dear, I hope you don't think when I said to thank me that I meant...!"

"Well, no, but now that you mention it...!" I shoved him over the side of the bed and he landed on the floor with a heavy thump.

"Sophie!" he yelled with a hurt voice as I laughed. His dignity and sense of humor sometimes clashed and when I'd do something a little rough or laugh at him when he wanted to be serious, his nose would get a little out of joint. But a little kiss always smoothed him down. But sometimes I'd catch a wary look in his eyes when he got serious and, he'd warn me, "Now, So, don't get mischievous." It was more fun to keep him just a little off-guard because, in too many things, he had the drop on me.

9. Like A Girl In Love...

That David loved me but that he also loved his wife was a fact I had to accept. It was never my intention to try to take David away from her, my desire was to have part of him for myself. We made each other happy, that was all I cared for.

We loved together many times that summer. Often the cabin was our place, but once, on a gray, foggy day he made love to me behind a barrier of driftwood. The open air with the cloak and damp of the day only added to my desire for him.

At home I tried to be as I'd always been.

My brothers were suspicious. I'd been seen walking on the beach with David. I was happy and cheerful around the house, which was always clean. The flowerbed was bright and the vegetable garden came up well. This efficiency bothered Zack.

I was setting the table one evening and singing, when he demanded, "Sophie, what's the matter with you?"

"Why, Zack," I answered innocently, "nothings the matter with me. Don't you like my singing?"

"Stop acting so damn prissy! It ain't normal. Not for you it ain't."

Instantly I was on my guard. "What's so un-normal about singing?"

"It ain't the singing. It's the way you do it. Flouncing around here. Cleaning up all the time."

Willie got into it then. "Oh, leave her alone, Zack. She's just happy. Nothin' wrong with that."

"I'm not so sure. What's she got to be so happy about? Living here on this lonely beach doing our washing and cleaning? Is that enough to make a woman sing? I don't remember our mother singing and working."

Neither Willie nor I answered him. I was hoping the whole thing would blow over before Zack thought anymore. Then, slyly, he slipped it in, "You act like a girl in love."

I couldn't deny it, but I wasn't about to admit it either. I tried to divert him. "Sure, Zack, I'm in love! With cooking your stupid meals and washing your stinking clothes. And I just love the thanks I get. Do you ever appreciate it? No, all you do is complain about the lousy three bucks a week I keep."

It worked. At the mention of the three dollars he jumped up, shouting, "It's more than three bucks, Missy! You get a buck fifty apiece from us each week and then grab another three bucks apiece for us. Supposedly. How do we know what you're doing with it?"

"Wait a minute, Zack!" Willie decided to defend me. "That's for our own good."

"I don't like it," Zack said, "It's my money and I never see it." While they argued I got the box with the bags from my bedroom. I'd started out with envelopes but that hadn't worked for very long as the cash started to pile up. So I made up three different bags for the money. I loved the feel and the sound of the money rustling around in the bags when I pulled the box from under my bed.

Willie's voice was loud. "You know we'd just blow it if she didn't keep it for us!" I came back and handed them their bags. Zack dumped his on the table and counted it. $96.00. Not a great sum nowadays but a comfortable amount for then.

Willie handed me back his bag. He didn't even open it. "I want you to still keep it for me, Sophie. If you don't I'll just waste it. I'll be going home in a month and if Nettie will have me, I want to marry her."

I knew Nettie, a girl who went to school with Willie, and I hoped, for his sake, that she would marry him. She came from a farm nearby where we bought pigs every spring to fatten and slaughter for winter.

She was prettier than any other girl around and was in a couple plays in school. I remembered especially once when we were over there and she took me into the house to show me the quilt she was working on. She had told me she'd like to join up with some people in Portland she knew about who put on, "real plays."

I also knew that she did like Willie, better'n he knew, but I wondered about her, could she be a good wife to him? Recalling that day at her place I didn't remember any big statements from her about how she was looking forward to settling down and cooking and cleaning for someone for the rest of her life. She made an impression on me because I'd had those thoughts but she was the first other girl I knew who actually talked about doing something else. But I couldn't see how she would really do what she talked about so I figured it wasn't something I needed to bring Willie's attention to. She was a good girl and I supposed she'd get over that stuff if she married Willie. So I kept my mouth shut and my doubts to myself.

"Sure, Willie," I agreed, "she'll like you even better for having money to get started." I knew that was true, she'd also said she didn't want to be a poor farmer's wife, which could mean that she was willing to be a well-off farmer's wife, I truly didn't know.

Zack shoved the money in his pocket and threw the bag down on the floor, then he picked it back up. "I been needing something to put my shoe stuff in, I'll just take this after all."

Things were all calmed down and we were eating dinner and Zack was planning the good time he'd have with his money, the girls he'd dance and romance, when he remembered.

"Who could the guy be?"

"What guy?" asked Willie. If he'd had any sense he'd have kept quiet but he was too busy eating meatloaf and boiled taters to be thinking.

"The guy Sophie's goofy over." He put his fork down and looked at me. "You haven't been to a dance in .. since Spring sometime." He nodded his head as he calculated time, moving his lips as he brought his focus on me. I felt a coldness along my spine and, touching the bowl of potatoes said to Willie, "Oh, I got a little bit of butter made today." He didn't even hear me. Zack had his attention.

"Aw, that don't mean nothin' Zack, Sophie's just too nice a girl for those roughnecks."

"Yeah?" He shook his head. "I'll take that butter." He smirked at Willie. "They weren't too rough for her before." A heat of anger and fear surged through me. I jumped up and grabbed the butter from the cooling shelf and slammed it down on the table beside Zack's plate. I wanted to slam him on the head with it but I'd worked too hard to ruin the butter. He didn't seem to notice my anger except for the smirk getting bigger on his face.

"Out with it Sophie girl, who is it?"

This time I was determined to stop it but it was beyond me. Standing over by the stove cleaning up the cooking mess I said, as casually as I could, seeing as I was blood-red mad, "There's nobody, Zack. It's just like Willie said, none of your pals are the kind of men I truly choose to be spending time with."

He looked at me then, and mimicked, "'Truly choose?'" and then slid into his regular voice, "Huh! It's my bet someone is feathering your nest right here. The hen don't have to wander far when she's got a rooster right close to home."

Both Willie and I stared at him, me because he had me nailed to the wall, Willie like Zack was speaking Chinese. I tried to distract him, "That's what I mean, crude talking like that! That's all you know, you and your pals...."

"Smithers?" Willie cut right through it. "You don't mean Smithers?" He stared at Zack who just shook his head at Willie like he was a simpleton.

"Of course I mean Smithers. Who else is around here? Not the 'rough' guys we work with! Oh no, it's that Fancy Dan with the smooth hands - and I'll bet he's smooth everywhere else too, eh, Sophie!" He leered at me. I felt my face go crimson.

The fire was hot in me. "Don't talk to me like that!"

48

Willie jumped up, outraged. "That's enough, Zack! Sophie's our sister, and Smithers is a married man! So they like to talk, that's no reason to get foul-mouthed about it. I know Smithers and he's a decent man! One more word like that and I leave! And Sophie goes with me!"

That startled me. I kept silent but, I had no intention of going anywhere. Willie's threat immediately calmed Zack down. Without me he'd be back to taking care of himself. He didn't want to do that.

"For God sakes, Willie, I was only kidding. Don't you know nothing? Sit down, eat your supper. Forget I said anything!" He took up the butter and started spreading some on his potatoes.

Willie looked at him and then at me. I shrugged my shoulders like what could we do with him, and motioned him to sit down at the table again. "Forget it, Willie. Finish your dinner. I've also got some pie tonight." He looked at me again and for one horrid moment I thought he was going to question me about David, then he shrugged his shoulders and sat back down.

"What kind of pie?" he asked, seriously, which would have made me laugh if I wasn't so frightened. I showed him the salal berry pie that I'd made in the cool of the morning with berries I'd picked the day before with David. He tucked into his dinner, a smile on his face.

We finished our meal in silence but Willie's words had been like a bucket of cold water thrown onto a forest fire. They didn't put out the flame I felt for David but I was more in control now. Willie was right, David was a married man. And I was beginning to suspect I was a pregnant woman. I felt disaster just around the corner. I was two weeks past my monthly, not usual for me. In another three weeks I'd know for sure.

10. What Am I Going To Do...?

My mind was clear, I must tell David. If I was pregnant I was no more than a month along. Maybe David would know what to do. Having a baby out-of-wedlock in those days was unthinkable. Shameful. I was terrified at the possibility.

The day after the argument I went to the beach in search of David. I found him near our log. He was happy to see me and hugged me hard and kissed me right there in the open. I hardly cared. "David, we've got to talk."

He knew something was very wrong. "Sure, honey, what's the matter?"

We sat on the log and I plunged right in. "I think I'm pregnant."

I certainly didn't expect him to leap up, laughing, reach down, grab me and yell, "Tremendous!" right in my face, but that's what he did! I was shocked, surprised.

"But, David," I tried to say. He didn't hear me.

"Are you sure? Oh, honey! This is wonderful! How far?" At last he was going to listen to me.

"You act like this is a glorious event! It's not! You're a married man. What's going to happen to me?" I could feel tears starting but I swallowed them.

"David, do you know anyway to stop it?"

He looked like I had struck him.

"You just put that idea out of your head right now! You could die!"

"David, you don't understand! What am I going to do?"

"Do?" He had the simplest explanation of all. "You'll come live with me, of course."

"With you? And what will Amy think of this fine idea." I thought he'd gone mad. Maybe he was "Crazy Smithers" after all!

"Why Amy thinks it's just fine!" He was as happy as a puppy let out to play, but I was thinking about what he'd just said.

"What do you mean Amy thinks it's just fine? She doesn't know about us, does she?"

He looked bewildered for a minute. "Sure, she knows. I couldn't keep something like this from her. She's known I love you since last spring, when we planted the roses." All I could think of was that David was off his rocker, and so was his wife.

"Look Sophie, maybe it does sound a little odd, but Amy and I ... we don't believe that a wedding band should cut you off from life. No one person can be everything to another. Amy loves the city, and plays, and crowded smoky rooms full of people. I hate it. So when she leaves in the summer she does all those things, with men who do enjoy them."

"Does she make love to them, like you do with me?" The whole idea was absurd, but I couldn't help asking. For a moment I ignored my predicament.

"No, she hasn't. It's just that it's her choice. So far she hasn't met any man she loves but me. But I'll understand if she does."

"But, David," I was repeating myself. "It's so dangerous. What if she finds someone, and leaves you?"

"Why ever should she leave me? The core of me is her and the core of her is me. That will never change! I know that as certain as I know that I love you and you love me. Do you doubt that I love you?"

"No." I didn't. I was absolutely certain.

"Ok. It's settled. Amy gets back the last week in September. We'll know for certain whether you're going to be a mother by then."

"David." It was time for some serious talking, of the way the world really is, not the way David wanted it to be. "This just won't work!"

"Sure.."

"No, wait. You've got some starry-eyed notion that Amy is just going to be delighted to welcome me into her home. She's not. I'll bet everything I have on it, which isn't much. She may be all you say. If she has allowed you to go with me .. knowing all about me .. then she is, well, unusual. I certainly wouldn't have left you alone here with me!"

For the first time he was concerned, "You're not a jealous woman, are you, So?"

That made me laugh, though it came out bitter. He was worried that I was a jealous woman!

"Frankly, I've never had the chance to find out. I've never really been in love, until you."

"How do you feel about Amy?" Finally, I'd gotten to him!

"I've got along with the idea of Amy because - I don't think about her! She's been gone all summer. It's like she doesn't exist. I never thought about Living with her! I can't believe even now that you would ever consider it. Why, she'd have to be a saint to do that!" Or nuts, I thought.

"The Mormons do it."

"What?"

"You know they do, and they get along all right. They don't think it's crazy."

"Maybe they don't but everybody else does!" I was suddenly suspicious. "You're not a Mormon, are you?" That would explain his crazy ideas.

"No, I'm not. But we grew up in Utah, so I've heard stories."

Then I remembered what he'd told me about his growing up, and I was relieved, let me tell you! An odd religion thrown in would have baked the cake.

"This whole thing is getting ahead of me. I'm getting a headache. Whatever happens I'm not moving into your house! It's just not natural!"

"I wouldn't force you to do something you think is wrong, but please, Sophie, at least think about it."

I promised to do that but I had no intention of giving in. I didn't want to meet Amy, nor even see her, let alone share her husband in the same house with her!

We parted without even a kiss. He tried but I wasn't feeling too well. I just wanted to go home, and lie down. He teased me then about, "Being just like a wife with headaches and no lovin'."

I didn't see anything to laugh about. I waved him away and trudged off through the sand. Walking up the path to the cabin I thought how easy it would be to slip, and fall, and lose the baby, but something else within me made me walk even more carefully, lest I fall and hurt the baby! I knew it was crazy thinking but I knew that if I was carrying a child, it was David's as well as mine, and he wouldn't want to lose another one.

When I got home I laid down for a while and after a while I felt better. Then I started thinking about Willie and Zack. The road job would close down at the end of September, about the same time Amy would be back. I still had no notion of living with them but I wanted to be close to David for as long as I could, no matter whether I was pregnant or not. Willie would be going home to Nettie - no problem there - but Zack was going to another construction job, in California, and was expecting me to go with him. I had to think of a believable reason for staying here in the cabin.

Telling him I was 'in trouble' was out of the question, but what if I told him that Amy was pregnant and that David had asked me if I could stay and help? No, not help. If Zack thought I could earn more money by staying rather than going with him ... he wouldn't like it, but he understood money.

But she'd been gone since late June. She couldn't be less than three months along. But did Zack know that most problems happen in the first three months? I was sure he didn't. Even so, there were other complications I could dream up.

After I got it satisfied in my mind that I could handle the boys, I put my thoughts to David. I had better get to know him even better. What did I really know about this man who might be the father of my child, and who had such strange ideas?

11. If He Only Knew...

David's father had been a Baptist minister in Virginia. When David was small his parents moved the family to Utah. Three families came with him from Virginia, all with equal purpose, to bring the True Word to the Mormon heathens. Their original goal had been Salt Lake City, but Preacher Smithers and his small, fervent group, found out within a week of arrival that, "The Devil had those people caught tightly in his talons," and Preacher Smithers decided the Lord was telling him that he hadn't meant Salt Lake City at all. Better to start small, perhaps some place where the Devil hadn't got such a firm hold.

Thus inspired they moved, hurriedly, as David remembered it, to a small town about fifty miles away.

They prayed and worked hard. After fifteen years the score was, BAPTISTS: one Lutheran family who changed over to "good Baptist Christians" mostly 'cause the little Baptist church was convenient, and one Mormon woman who was friendly so they had hope for her; and, MORMONS: nearly everybody else, including David's brother who married a Mormon girl, becoming an LDS convert and active worker for the "opposition". David married Amy about that time. She was from the Lutheran family.

Preacher Smithers was hearty in his approval of the marriage, considering the "disaster" that had befallen the eldest son. He encouraged David to move on to less soul-endangering surroundings. They feared the exposure of future grandchildren to the predominant religion. David would have left anyway, as he was filled with a longing for an ocean he'd never seen.

His success as a painter was slow, but he worked lumbering and part-time as a hired hand. They never starved, and David was content to remain by the sea for the rest of his life.

Their unusual ideas of life were a mixture of what they saw in their growing up, and from reading. David told me that there was more than one approach to life and marriage. He was determined not to get set in, "a mold. It makes moldy people," he would later tell me.

He had a bit of the preacher in him, too. Not in religious ways, but he loved to talk and could at times be most stubborn to have people agree with him. It was amazing to him that I, (and Amy), didn't immediately grasp the, 'truth' of his ideas. "But it's so clear!" he would shout.

That was always the end of the sermon because Amy would say, "Amen, David." He would purse his lips in annoyance, but stop.

But David's strongest holdover from his Father's influence was what he called his, "inability to swear properly." I first heard the expression, "cotton pickin' thunderbolts," when he went to push a stick further into a campfire and burned his hand on the fire in the coals. He dropped the stick and exploded with the oath. I laughed. I'd expected,'damnation!' at least, and told him so.

"I've tried." He was hurt at my laughter. "But it just doesn't work. I had it pressed in me hard as a youngster that only bad people swear. I never really believed it 'cause Amy's Dad seemed to get relief from a good, 'Damn!' now and then but other than that, I just didn't hear much swearing where I grew up. But I was willing to learn! After Amy and I left home, I worked with a lumber crew and practiced everything I heard (not around Amy of course). But, you know, Sophie, something was wrong." His eyebrows wrinkled in bewilderment.

"Every 'damn' came out sounding like 'darn' and 'Hell!' always made me nervous. The worse ones were beyond me. They stuck in my throat and sounded weak when they came out. The guys laughed at me. They called me ... oh, never mind that...."

I wanted to explore that but he got red so I let it be.

"I gave it up and went back to my old home words. I decided it's not what you say as much as how you say it. I get just as much satisfaction from a good, hearty 'Cottinpickin!' as Mr. Swenson did from his 'Damn'."

I think it was David's only defeat, except for me, and I wasn't a complete loss.

The next two weeks went on eternally. Every day after the boys left for work, David would stop at the cabin. We would have a cup of coffee and then go for a long walk on the beach or build a fire and sit and talk. One thing we didn't do in that two weeks was make love! I wanted to, he wanted to. But I stopped him, thinking, if I maybe wasn't with child we should quit while we still had the chance. Suddenly the chances I had taken seemed so foolhardy. I wasn't ignorant of the facts of life. But the passion I felt for David had swept all caution from my mind. For two weeks, we didn't do it.

We talked a lot but David never said he was sorry for making me pregnant, because he wasn't. He hoped I was. And I hoped I wasn't.

My monthly never came and my breasts got tender, and I threw up in the morning, two days in a row. The second morning, afterwards, I was sitting in front of the cabin on the bench that Willie had made. They were gone to work and I was being still, breathing in the cool of the morning, watching the fog lift over the sea, when David came down from his place and sat on the bench beside me. Zack and Willie had gone to work hours before, we were completely alone. Except I wasn't feeling alone. I knew I was growing a child within me.

I was happy to see David, I needed his comforting hands holding mine. And his words. "Hey, sweet," he said, softly, glancing at me with worried eyes, "What's up? Wanna walk?"

"In a minute." I shifted on the bench to face him, my view changing to the length of the beach. In the distance I could see a family of Mom, Dad, dog, and three children going toward the waves, the kids kicking at the sand, the dog leaping around them all.

"I wonder, David, with all your smarts, is this baby a boy, or a girl?" I watched his face. His white teeth showed as he grinned big. I remember that moment so clearly. He swallowed, hard. I reached out and touched his Adam's apple, just a light stroke. He reached up and took my hand and put my fingers to his mouth, kissed them.

"Oh, a boy would be nice this time, or a girl, one or the other. You choose." He leaned his head back and closed his mouth, just laughing from deep inside. I snuggled into him, not caring who might see. He put his arm around me. "Wanna walk?"

"Yes, indeed. We've been waiting for you." I felt full to bursting over, full of energy and love and a need to move. He jumped from the bench, nearly upending it. I almost fell the length of it, he grabbed me and lifted me up, grinning.

"Race you - oh, I guess not." I dashed past him and down the path, not running full tilt but keeping ahead of him. "Not fair,' I heard him say through running breaths.

"I never said I was fair." I got to the water first, he let me to be sure, but I enjoyed my triumph. For just a minute he took my hand and we walked that way a few feet before he remembered my need for caution and let it go. I just sighed, confused with both happiness and sadness, but for that morning, happiness won out.

David had enough sense not to dance around when we were sure. He was just quietly happy. The corners of his mouth would twitch with a held-back grin when he looked at me. He took to patting my belly and breasts in a pleased and protective way. At first it annoyed me, but his joy was catching. And I was never one to mope for long about something I could do nothing about.

The last week before Amy came home we made our plan. David arranged with the landlady for me to continue to rent the cabin. He told her that I would be staying to help with his wife. I told the same story to Zack and Willie. I don't think Zack believed it but he kept his thoughts to himself. He didn't care what happened to me as long as he wasn't around to be shamed. He left for California a week before Willie was to go home.

Willie was outside and Zack was leaving. He turned to me at the door and said, nastily, "I do hope you've had fun!" He looked from my face to my belly, and left. It shook me and I was afraid he'd say something to Willie but when Willie came back he was all smiles as usual. That was on Sunday.

Wednesday morning David stopped for his coffee. He asked how the quilt was coming along. I knew it was an excuse to get into my bedroom. I hadn't worked much on the quilt for the last three weeks. I pulled him behind the curtain where he took me gently in his arms. "So?" he asked.

"Yes, please." His touch on my back was a welcome fire.

We lay down on the bed, close together. He was leaning over me, kissing me with his hand stroking my belly when the curtain flew back and there was Willie, a look of murder on his face. I think if he'd actually caught us making love he'd a killed us both.

"So, Zack was right!" he yelled. Before we could move he'd pulled David off the bed and flung him on the floor like a feather. He stood for a second staring at me still on the bed. I was so scared.

"You're no better'n a whore!"

David wasn't a fighter, that wasn't his way, but at that moment he'd have killed Willie or died trying, before he let me be harmed. He jumped up, both his hands flexing, balling into fists and flattening out in front of him at Willie.

"Get out of here!" The words snapped from him to Willie with the force of a whip. His cold anger shocked Willie and stopped him long enough for me to roll off the bed and at least die standing up. Don't think I didn't think of rolling under the bed, but as much as I longed for a rock to crawl under, I feared David was in danger of being beaten to death by my strong ox of a little brother. I dodged past them and ran into Willie's room where I got his deer rifle, which he always kept loaded.

When I got back David was on the floor , blood streaming from his nose. Willie raised his boot and I knew for certain he'd stomp him to death.

"You touch him again and I'll shoot you right now," I said, pointing the gun straight at him.

Willie stopped in midair. I meant it, and he knew it. David knew it, too. He staggered up.

"For God's sake, Sophie!" David almost fell into me. "Don't! Don't shoot!" His voice was rough, raw, almost like crying. He was so afraid I'd do it before he could stop me.

All the fight went out of Willie. His face flexed as he pulled in his anger, turned away from us, ripped roughly at the bedroom curtain and pushed through it to stumble to the kitchen table. He jerked a chair out and almost fell into it.

We followed him and stood nearby watching him closely. He was crying. "I don't understand, I don't understand." David reached outward and put a hand on his shoulder.

"Willie, Sophie and I love each other." Willie's shoulder jerked to throw off David's hand.

"Love!" He spat out. He made it sound like a dirty word. "A married man loves his wife." He turned, glaring, to me. "And to think I stood up for you when Zack had it figgered out all along. If he only knew!"

He and I had always been close so it shattered me to hear him talk like that. The mention of Zack was like sea water on a fresh wound. I didn't care what Zack thought of me, but I knew I could never go home again if Willie told Mom and Dad, or anybody in the family. There'd be no way to ever explain David and I. None of the sisters would have ever trusted me with their husbands again, though they needn't have worried. In the Elm's no one played around with married people.

As for the baby, I'd already cooked up a story about a quick romance with a fisherman after Willie left. After a mythical wedding, and the baby had come, he would conveniently drown in a storm on a fishing boat. It was a wild idea, and now I realize, very thin, but it was the only chance I had of saving any face at all. The baby would have to be explained, sooner or later, but I didn't intend for it to be this way.

"Willie, you must never tell him! You must never tell anybody! They'd never understand! They'd hate me! You know it!"

I got to him with the wildness of my appeal. He glared at me for a long time. "Ok, Sophie. But it's the last favor I ever do for you."

Abruptly, he stood up.

David put a protective arm around my shoulders.

"You needn't worry," Willie said, sadly, the fight gone from him. "I'm through with the both of you. I'm going home."

He went to his room where he threw everything he owned into his old bag. I got his savings and before he went out the door, handed the moneybag to him. He looked at it queerly, then opened it, took the money out and stuffed it into his old bag. He dropped the empty bag onto the floor.

"I forgot my lunch," he said, then went out, closing the door firmly behind him.

"Forgot his lunch? Whatever did...?" I wondered, aloud.

David pointed to Willie's lunch pail, still on the table where I set it for him every morning. We hadn't even noticed it.

12. But, It's All Arranged...

Maybe it was my condition .. after Willie left the tears started. I cried 'till I thought my heart would crack or my guts fall out. It hurt. All the fear I'd held bottled up came out in one great gush. Something dried up in me that day. Only one more time was I to cry so deeply, and even then....

After it was done, I was drained, like a stone, cold and lifeless. If anything was going to shake out that baby that day ought to have done it. But, thank God, it didn't.

David worried about me. He stayed with me the next few days 'till Amy came home. He coddled me like a beloved sick child, bringing me tea with honey in it, cooking soup, trying to make me laugh. Finally, somehow, I came back to life again, to myself. It was impossible, with David around, to stay gloomy too long. He was like life itself, always positive that things would turn out for the best.

He stayed at the cabin with me until it was time to go pick up Amy. I dreaded his leaving, afraid I'd never see him again. I knew that if I was Amy and he suggested to me what he was about to suggest to her, that my reaction would be to get him away from there as fast as I could, or demand that I go. And knowing that Amy's hold on him was longer and stronger than mine, she just might be able separate us.

That's one of the reasons I told him I would not agree to live with him and Amy. If she was half the woman David said she was, she just might be able to put up with me at a distance, unseen. The truth? I couldn't imagine facing her. Willie's reaction had been so severe against me, and he was my own flesh and blood. What might hers be?

Amy held all the cards. With one word she could stop David in his happy tracks, and destroy me as well. She had only to say, "No," for I wouldn't fight for him. If he'd ever given the slightest hint that he was unhappy with Amy, I would have. But he never suggested leaving her, it never even occurred to him. It was more than the fact that that people seldom got divorced in those days, she was part of him. They were like the alternating threads in a piece of fabric, together they made a whole. If I had tried to replace her I'd have had to unwind them first and it would have weakened David. I loved him too much for that.

During the time David stayed with me I managed to undermine his confidence in his happy plan enough to squelch some of his so-obvious glee. It annoyed the hell out of me that he was so fearless, and it seemed to me, unrealistic. Thus, when he left, he at least had some fear of Amy's reaction!

I don't think I slept a wink all night. I walked the floor, and drank coffee. For a while the slice of moon lit the surf but then clouds moved in and the moon moved on down the sky, making the night even darker. I was grateful for the dawn, to give up the pretense of sleeping. I made oatmeal and toast for breakfast and only nibbled the toast. I made bread more for the work of it, to have something to do, than because I needed it. I kneaded and pounded that dough until it all the air bubbles were popped and the surface was shiny. Might have been the best bread I ever made!

By the afternoon I knew I'd never see David again. My palms were sweaty, my heart feeling heavy in my chest. I could feel it pounding. With every outside noise I went to the door and opened it, until I gave up and settled at the kitchen table. The bread had risen and baked and I'd even eaten a piece of it. I watched the waves surge in and out, the surf breaking with the white foam against the gray of the autumn ocean. I sat with my hands in my lap, not trying to busy them or my mind. Waiting. I was watching the clouds lighten as the sun set behind them when I heard David's knock on the door. My hands flew up and settled again in my lap before I was able to say, "Come in, David."

He came in all smiles. His first words were, "Are you ready?"

Ready for what: to be shot? killed? maimed in some horrible way by an outraged wife? I was too stunned to speak. He realized that he'd been abrupt. He put his arms around me, lifting me to stand with his arms around me, my head on his shoulder. "Everything's all right. I told you it would be."

I couldn't believe it.

"Come on, she wants to meet you."

At that, I pulled back. "Never!"

"Don't be silly, how are you going to live with us without ever meeting Amy?" He thought he had everything solved because he had been able to get one woman to agree to his crazy scheme.

I was suddenly so weary that I had to sit down. He was looking around like he was deciding what I should bring with me.

"I told you before that I wouldn't live with you."

His forehead wrinkled and his eyes grew wide. "But Sophie, it's all arranged."

"Don't 'But Sophie' me! To have Amy agree to me even being in the same country with you is enough for me. I don't want to meet her, I couldn't face her. And I doubt..."

He interrupted me. "You're getting upset for...."

"that she really wants to meet me," I finished.

He couldn't budge me. He finally had to accept it. That's the way it stayed for the next five months.

13. A Bit of Fluff

David visited every day. Amy sent books for me to read, though I wasn't much of a reader. She sent soup and bread once in a while which I ate, because David saw to it that I did. He and I went for walks when the weather wasn't too stormy, me all bundled up like a mummy.

I was uncomfortable outside. Amy had the advantage of being able to see me, to watch me through that telescope. David insisted she wasn't watching me, but I knew she could if she wanted to. I would have.

The first month being alone wasn't so bad. October, a wonderful month along the coast. But, as winter set in, and dragged on - oh, the loneliness. It got terrible. The rain wasn't too bad, at least it was something to watch, but the everlastin' fog beat me. It curled up and settled around the cabin, at first like a cozy blanket; it became like a prison. Nothing but gray everwhich way I looked. The continual roaring of the winter ocean got on my nerves. When the big storms would come the waves would smack against each other with a loud crack! then thunder down on the sand. It was exhilarating when there was someone to share it with; alone it frightened me. Even with no storm there was always that noise of the water moving. I began to understand why Amy didn't go down anymore.

When David was with me I didn't hear the ocean and it didn't matter what the weather was outside. He came for lunch every day, bringing groceries and newspapers and gossip from town. The two hours he stayed became the only part of the day worth getting up for.

The thing that saved my sanity, I'm sure, was the company of Punkin Sue Tiger, a golden kitten David gave me for Halloween. David came late one afternoon, near evening, his hands behind his back.

"Close your eyes and put out your hands," he insisted. I didn't feel comfortable doing that since one of my brothers handed me a snake that way once. After promising I would like the surprise, I yielded, as I did in so many things to him.

The moment he put this little warm bundle of fur into my hands my eyes snapped open. It was the cutest thing - a furry kitten, about six weeks old. He squeaked when I lifted him up close, then started purring when I laid him on my shoulder. The more I petted him the louder his purrs got. Like David's grin, Punkin Sue Tiger's purring captured my heart.

David said I should keep him inside the cabin but Punkin Sue Tiger wasn't an indoor cat. After David left, the kitten followed me around the cabin. I warmed up a bit of milk and put it in front of him but he only drank a little before, with tiny mews, he was exploring the cabin again.

I named him Punkin Sue Tiger because of his color and the fact we didn't know what sex he was. We thought he was a she, thus Sue, after a particularly catty woman I knew up home. In the evening I sat in the chair looking out the window at the ocean. Punkin Sue Tiger came up and began playing at my bare toes trying to grab them as I rocked. He made more happy little mews as I picked him up to avoid the rocker's legs, he settled right down on my lap as I stroked his yellow fur. Mixed in with the pumpkin color were a few darker, tiger stripes. His little body just vibrated while I petted him. I pulled lightly on his tail, he turned around and looked at me in such a way that I stopped, but then I just couldn't help myself, I did it again. This time that little thing growled at me! Like most guys he didn't much like me to laugh at him, but he wasn't serious enough about it to get off my lap.

When I went to bed I put him in a box padded with rags, but after a couple of "meows" I got up and put him on the cover beside me, the top quilt edge turned back over him to keep him warm.

When I woke up he was still beside me, but snuggled under the covers, his whiskers tickling at my chin. His bright eyes were staring at me, his little mouth was open, crying at me to get up. He was too small to get off the bed without falling. I took him outside with me for his morning walk and he seemed as happy to get back in the warm house as I was.

He delighted me, he was something to talk to, and play with, and care about. And he gave me no complicated arguments!

I did spoil him terrible so that he crawled up the chair and hung around my neck like a fox fur when I was sewing, or, once in a great while, reading a paper. The rattle of the paper teased him like a mouse and he'd swipe at it with his tiny claws. Later he got to be a real nuisance with the embroidery thread but no matter what he did, he kept me from suffering more.

14. The Quilt and a Letter

Without the boys I had a lot of time on my hands. I took over their room for sleeping and turned mine into a sewing place and took back up with the quilt. David helped with more drawings of patterns for the rocks. He had strong ideas about the colors I should use. Even wanted to bring me some blue material Amy had that he said would be just right for the water where it met the sky but I wasn't having any of her material in my quilt. It was our quilt, I didn't want any of her in it.

From a sheet that Willie had left behind I made a bag into which I put all the material that would go into 'Beach'. I lugged the old one into the front room where the fire warmed me and the light from the window brightened my dark mood. Bringing out all the old materials brought up the past, everything seemed so simple then, now my life was a tangle. The ocean moved slowly in large swells; sometimes I would just sit and stare at it, watching the birds flying in and out of the thin fog, then I'd go back to sorting material.

I usually made pieced quilts, 'Beach' was an appliqué, you know, small pieces sewn onto to a larger piece to make a design. Beach was the first one I ever did that way, and even with David's help I still frustrated myself over the colors. There were the brown and gray leftovers from Zack's quilt, and some blue. More of Zack ended up in Beach than I planned but as I worked on the quilt I forgot the bad things and only remembered that first night when he went poetic on us and so what had been a bad memory eased into pleasant.

Large chunks of gray from a wool army blanket that he'd got from somebody who brought it back from the war - it was darker than I liked but what the heck, the Army hadn't asked me before dyeing their blankets. It would do well for the frame around the frontpiece.

I separated out the rich light blue of a cotton blanket that I'd used for Zack's border and as a runner between the squares. I loved the color which reminded me of the eyes of a Siamese cat a neighbor had had. Of course it didn't have the see-through quality that the cat's eyes had had, but it was a lovely shade of blue. There was a lot of it. I'd only cut from the sides leaving me about half a blanket, good for the deeper ocean behind the rocks. I'd have liked more. Greedy? I made do with what I had. There was even some left over - you might remember it from the Name Quilt?

The leftovers from Willie were fewer and smaller but that was ok because so much of 'Ocean' was of drab grays and deeper blues. The little spots of color stood out and brightened it in a way that a fully-colored design wouldn't have. For the lighthouse I found an especially clear emerald green, perfect for the sea around the base. I think it was left over from the collar of a cousin's flower girl dress. A yellow that came from a piece I'd bought special for a quilted pillow I made for Mandy's wedding present - it fit for the lighthouse beam - just a tiny spot but a pleasant memory for me every time I saw it.

So many other bits of color scavenged from aprons I'd made for Christmas presents for Mom and my sisters over the years. Tiring of pulling them out piece by piece I upended the bag onto the floor. I didn't have much money but I was rich in material! Calicos and stripes and prints along with plain blacks, blues, and greens. Not much extra yellow because I used it so much in my quilts. Every bit of fabric took me back to an easier time.

I pulled out a bright orangeish-yellow from the skirt I'd made Mandy when she was pregnant with one of the first kids. She never liked it so was happy to donate it to my quilt bag when I'd packed to go to the beach with the boys. That seemed so long ago! The orange was perfect for the starfish clinging to the rocks at the base of Haystack. I smoothed the material flat, my heart filling with a bittersweet feeling. I'd used that color in every one of the stars in Willie's quilt, with a narrow band of it around the outside for a frame. It was so cheerful! It had taken a lot of piecing because I'd cut it sparingly, not wasting one scrap.

The pieces laid in a heap while I stared out at the ocean, noting the tide line and the little birds skittering along the edge picking up broken bits of clam or tiny bits of fish. I knew that if I was close up I would hear their little cheeps sounding like baby chicks calling to their mother.

I got on with the job, tossing back into the old bag the patterns leaving only the plain for the front of the quilt.

Every day I pulled the bag into the front room and settled myself into the chair between the table and the window. It took days to get the pieces cut just right. And more weeks to get them pinned onto the large curtain piece that David bought new from Puffing, a large plain piece of cotton but of substantial strength to hold the appliqué.

The day he brought it he also carried with him a letter. I saw it poking out from his jacket but was excited about the cloth, and planning how I'd dye it a pale blue as backdrop for the sea and sky. I didn't know the letter was for me. I made us tea while we talked about how to use the cloth when suddenly he slapped his forehead with the palm of his hand.

"Oh, I forgot! When I picked up the material today from Puffing he gave me this letter for you."

He handed it to me and I was staring at my name written in Mandy's big scrawly handwriting on the front. I felt the letter and held it up to the light from the window and rubbed it and flattened it. It was pretty thin.

"Guess she doesn't have much to say," I said and put the envelope on the table.

"Aren't you going to open it?"

"Well, sure. But I thought we could drink our tea first."

"Sophie! How long has it been since you heard from your family?"

"Well, that's kind of just it. Maybe I don't want to. Maybe Zack or Willie told them something about, well, you know. Us. Maybe my brothers told my mother about you and me. Maybe Mama has figured out that I'm not just staying as a housekeeper for the neighbors."

"If you don't open it you'll never know."

"Maybe I'd rather not know!" He was always pushing at me!

"Ok, Sophie. I've got to get back to the house. I'd sure be interested to know what your sister has to say, when you finally read it. You will open it, won't you?"

"Uh huh." I picked up the cotton material and started folding it.

He left and I messed around with the pieces that I'd cut out with David's design, opening the material back up and trying pieces on it to see how'd they look. I'd still have to wash and iron it, and dye it, but I needed to try it out first. I pinned Haystack Rock just to the left of center, a bit below the halfway mark so there'd be room for the tide pools. Haystack was a perfect reddish brown, like it is when the sunset turns the sky red. The two thumbs out of the same cloth went to either side. At the place of the tide pools I pinned on the smaller rocks and attached some of the starfish and anemones and pieces of tide pool plants. David had found a sand-colored piece onto which he'd drawn the little birds that skittered over the sand in that way they had that I loved. On another piece he'd drawn seagulls.

The letter sat on the end of the table where I'd pushed it to make room for the pieces. I forgot, almost, that it was there, until it started getting too dark for the close work I had to do. When I went to fold up the cloth to put it away the letter got knocked to the floor. I left it there while I put everything back in the sewing chest where Punkin Sue Tiger couldn't get at it.

I made another cup of tea and put another piece of wood in the stove and stirred the beans I was cooking for dinner, all the while thinking about every possible thing that Mandy could have to say, going back and forth from things the boys could have told her, to telling myself that the letter wouldn't have anything to do with me, to worrying that maybe something had happened to somebody in the family - Mother or Daddy? I finally sat down at the table with the letter and used my pocketknife to open it.

She didn't have the best handwriting but it was clear. She wanted to bring the kids down to the ocean and visit with me. Would I have room for them in the cabin? She didn't have money to spare to rent a cabin but would bring enough of her canned food to help out while she was there and she'd thought from what I'd said in the letter I'd sent several months back that we could get clams and fish enough from the ocean that we'd all have enough to eat. Maybe we could make clam chowder?

Here? She was going to come here? I could barely breathe as I thought about it. I'll tell you, Annie, I never wrote a letter back to someone so fast in my life! Of course most of it was a lie! It had to be! I couldn't tell her the truth. I ate some beans and bread while I thought about what to say. Before I went to bed I'd written my letter telling her that I was now living in the house with the Smither's family 'cause the wife needed me in the house and that the cabin was rented out to another family and that as much as I'd love to see them, this spring just wasn't going to be a good time because the wife would be having a baby sometime around then but that her mother would probably be coming sometime and then, maybe?

For once I was glad my family didn't have money for vacations and like that. I'm ashamed at how easy it was to lie to her and how easy it all came out of me that way. But, it worked. She wrote back saying she was sorry and the children had really been looking forward to it which I thought was silly because they didn't know anything about the ocean and were still little enough to not care about going someplace but I figured that was Mandy's way of telling me how disappointed she was.

I was relieved. The day I got the first letter from her was just a terrible shock and the second letter was a great relief! The time in between was awful.

Sewing the frontpiece of 'Ocean' kept me busy, a joy as I was making this with David. But most of the time I was alone and I could feel my belly growing larger with the week. I'd see little poke- outs on my tummy when I was sitting - his foot as he stretched his leg - an elbow when he turned - this baby was telling me he needed more

77

room! I would shift and the bump would go away but it would remind me that he, or she! was growing and was going to have to come out someday. I'd break out in a sweat when I remembered Mandy's birthings. She hadn't had any bad trouble, but I could see that it wasn't a comfortable experience. Hadn't bothered me when it was her - it was different now that it was me.

When I made the backside of the quilt I changed my mind about the solid gray pulling out the patterned materials that I'd stuffed back into the bag. The old cloth with the family memories gave me comfort. Everybody had troubles - most made it through. I made large squares of crazy quilt and joined them together. When I closed up the whole thing I made a frame for both front and back from the gray of Zack's Army blankets. Later, with Amy I embroidered yellow suns around the edges.

I was pregnant, I was alone, I was afraid, and I despaired that David would ever be mine. The nights were long and so lonely. But, like everything else, I lived through it. The change when it came took me by surprise, though why I can't say now, as I should have been expecting it. David usually did get what he wanted.

15. Tonight, He's Yours

The more bored and lonely I got the more David insisted I come with him and Amy. I was strong willed, but, I tell you, Annie, to me nothing was worse than that continual fog and rain. If I'd been well, maybe I could have stood it, but I had heartburn, my legs cramped up at night, my back ached and I was so bloated I felt about to bust sometimes. Still I might of stuck it out 'till the baby was born if I hadn't fallen.

I was coming back from the woodshed, my arms full of wood for the fire for David's lunch when I slipped on the dang eel grass and landed flat on my rump. I didn't hurt myself but David was just coming down from his place and saw me fall. He helped me up and made sure I was all right but didn't say anything about it. That should have been a warning because David could carry on something fierce about the littlest problems I had.

That evening there was a light knock on the door. I thought David was being gentle because he didn't want to disturb me in case I was asleep.

When I opened the door a woman was standing there - I knew immediately that it was Amy. She stepped into the room. She was not a timid woman. Right off I sensed the power and downright good sense of her. She was shorter than me, but not little. That night she had on a dark green cape that showed that her eyes were more hazel than the brown that Willie had described. She fixed them on me as she used one foot to push the door shut behind her while she was untying her cape. The hood fell back and she shook her hair to lift the blond curls of her bangs up from where the cape had flattened them. I guess her hair had grown since Willie had seen her on the beach with David. She'd pulled it up into a soft bun from which some strands had escaped, falling down onto her shoulders. She was a pretty thing.

She took the cape off and laid it over the back of one of the kitchen chairs. Of all things she was wearing a crème colored silk blouse that she'd tucked neatly into a tailored brown skirt. She was wearing pearls, for Pete's sake! Dressed to kill - only time I ever saw her dressed like that (usually she wore her hair in braids and plain cotton clothes for working around the house). She was sensible though, her shoes were the sturdy black oxfords she favored. She wouldn't have slipped coming down the path from their place.

I'd moved over back up against the table when she reached for me. I couldn't move.

"Dear Sophie," she said as she took my hand. 'Dear'? She plunged to the point. "David tells me you fell today. Certainly you know you cannot be alone any longer! It's totally unnecessary." The small movements on my part to pull my hand from her grasp were ignored.

"David wants you with us..."

"Did he send you?" I was angry at this woman. And David. She was upsetting all my notions about her. I preferred to think of her, when I allowed myself to think of her at all, as a woman desperate for her husband's love. A woman willing to do as he bid her. A meek, submissive little nobody who secretly hated me but desperately kept it from David with her soups and sweet inquiries about my health.

"No. He didn't." She released my hand. "When I told him I was coming he tried to stop me, and then he wanted to come with me - but the talk we must have can't be done with him around. Now," she sat down, almost completely at ease. She motioned me to do the same. That irritated me, it was, after all, my house. In an odd way of defiance I chose to sit, but on the edge of my chair, to show I would do as I pleased in my own home, not as she bid me. I wanted her to know that I was not as mallable as she. "I understand from David that you think his idea of us all living together is crazy, perhaps immoral. Gosh, I hope you're not right, but, as you know, David isn't like other men. That's why I love him so. If we're going to make this all turn out so that no one gets hurt - well, no more than can be helped - well, we're going to have to do something unusual to you and me than what either of us would think of. And we have the baby to think of."

I sat quiet, no words in me, as she explained what she wanted me, us, to do, and why. Punkin Sue Tiger lay curled up behind the door, among my boots and clamming gear, waiting for the stranger to go away, his eyes fixed on the woman as she talked.

"For as long as I've known him David has approached things with a different eye than most other people. He proposed to me when he was seven and I was only five. Even then I knew he was different. He'd watch everything everyone did and knew instinctively which things made people happy and what tormented them. He had a reverence for marriage and love that you probably find confusing, considering the circumstances you find yourself in. But David knows that the only way to hold a love is with open arms. There is the danger your mate will fly away, yes, but what's sadder than the eyes of an animal caught in a trap? I've seen it in the eyes of too many people wedded for life to their one-and-only."

She almost made sense. I thought of my sister Amanda and her husband, of my Mom and Dad. I'd seen the look. But I'd never known what caused it. Maybe Amy and David were right. I never knew a happier married couple.

"Maybe it makes a little more sense to you now," she saw my hand trying to cover the big belly that seemed to me to fill the room, "but, that is not the point right now.

"If you don't move up with us, one of us will have to come down here and be with you." She was stating it as a fact, unquestioned. She wasn't asking if I agreed. I could have argued. I could have refused, like I had with David, but what good would it have done? I'd still have had to see them every day -both of them - I was sure Amy wouldn't let me be now.

Before I gave in I had a question that had been bothering me from David's first mention of me living with them. Her frankness made me bold. Ok, I might live with them, but, "where — where would I ...?"

Amy raised her eyebrows, and finished my question, "Where would you sleep?"

I felt my face flush. I looked over her shoulder, at the wall, at the dark window, at Punkin Sue Tiger peeking out from between my beach boots. Everywhere but at her, especially not at the clear gaze of her eyes. If I thought my stomach seemed big before, now it was gigantic, the only thing in the room. She knew I was embarrassed, she just shrugged her shoulders.

"Frankly," and she laughed a little shakily, "that has bothered me. Too. But I think that if we face it head on we'll be ok." Quickly, as if to get the pain over as fast as possible, like ripping off a cover over a sore, she told me I'd be sleeping in what had been the storage room, that it was all ready for me with my own bed, and had been for weeks. As for where David slept, the only way to prevent, "problems, between us, is to share him."

"You know," again that quiet laugh, "this is the first time I've ever had to actually practice what David, and I, preach. I hope you'll help me."

I was anxious to have her keep talking, I nodded yes. She was uncomfortable. She rose and stood at the window and stood looking out into the now-dark night.

"David will spend one night with you, the next with me, and then with you again." She took a deep breath, "and so on." She turned toward me again. No tears. There was a sadness in her eyes that had not been there before. I suppose she'd dealt with her own devils long before tonight. With a quick sigh the look was gone; I only saw it once again.

Oddly, it was that quick look of sadness that convinced me. Up 'til then I'd feared that Amy, like David, saw no pitfalls in this scheme. She knew as well as I, the dangerous thing we were attempting, but she was willing, for David's sake, and the baby's, to give it all she had.

And I knew at that moment with an intuition rare to me, that she would do whatever she needed to do to save her marriage. That's when I put away the last, small hope I had that I could wiggle David away from her.

I was lighter, my belly felt normal, baby-sized again. It took little effort to go to her, take her hands in mine and say, "Ok. We'll do it." She knew I meant she and I, not David. She squeezed my hands, sealing our bargain. I pulled my hands away, wanting now to get this closeness over with.

Together we got my nightclothes and a few toilet articles. She went to the door, I hesitated a moment, then blew out the lamp and followed her. It was dark, and slippery. This way was new to me. She reached around, took my hand and led me up the path. The surf pounded below us, the only sound in an otherwise soundless night. The only light in our dark world came from the house she was leading me to. My mind was spinning.

I realized we'd left Punkin Sue Tiger in the house and started to turn back to get him. She misunderstood my move and tightened her grip. I didn't explain, he'd be all right tonight, I could get him in the morning.

The morning! The night! Right now, I didn't know which I feared more.

I concentrated on the sound of the waves landing on the sand to avoid what she was leading us to. My instinct was to turn and run; Amy's hand tightened on mine. The light from the house grew brighter as we got closer.

Just as we got to the door Amy stopped and, through a fog of near-panic, I heard her say, "Tonight, he's yours."

She gave me no time to answer, her hand turned the doorknob, and with her palm strong on my back, we entered her home, together."

End of Part One

Threads

Part Two

16. Names on a Quilt

Once Aunt Sophie started reliving the days of sixty years ago it was as if her dammed up memory started flooding. She continued talking as we picked the rest of the berries, took them home, washed and picked them over.

From the basement I could hear her talking while I packed a few boxes with empty jars. Upstairs she interrupted her story only to direct me in scrubbing the dusty jars and sterilizing them in boiling water to make them ready for the bubbling jam. We put up 14 jars and had enough leftover to make 3 small pies for the freezer.

The kitchen was small and old-fashioned, like the house. It belonged to my Uncle Boyd, the fifth child of Amanda's whom Aunt Sophie had declared would probably turn out to be undependable, a roving artist perhaps. He certainly would not be the one to support Amanda in her old age.

He delighted Aunt Sophie by walking and talking early, he became her favorite nephew. Because he was her favorite, and perhaps reminded her of her own child, she had given him more attention and was harder on him than any of the others. As he grew, and a talent for drawing and comedy became more an more pronounced, she encouraged, and some say, harassed him to apply himself to his talents and his studies. Through her influence he finished high school two years early and then to her dismay, he left home, or fled, to wander about the country, picking up work where he could.

Boyd had a curiosity about people, that, coupled with a fascination about how they governed their lives led him to watching more closely the activities of those who are entrusted with power to govern for all: politicians. He sought jobs with small town newspapers and his knack for discovering who really ran what, and why, and reporting it clearly and humorously in succinct cartoons, led him to Washington where he drew his cartoons for the most loved or most hated paper in the Capitol.

Nationally famous, he turned homeward to the person responsible for developing his close observation of people, his discipline, and his unwavering honesty - Aunt Sophie. On one of his trips home he decided to buy a parcel of Oregon to come home to, he said, and found the small house with a few apple trees, plum and peach trees, and edging the property, blackberries. There was also a Royal Ann cherry tree, and a pear. A small stream ran through the back. Aunt Sophie fell in love with the place so Uncle Boyd asked her if she would do him a favor, live in it and take care of it for him. There's no doubt in me that he planned it all along.

She moved in and lived there for close to twenty-five years. On the rough walls of the outhouse she pasted quotations by Thoreau, pictures cut from magazines, many of the sea, and poems that she liked. Robert Service's "The Cremation of Sam Magee" was a favorite.

"The Cremation" filled much of the door and the relatives said such silliness just proved Sophie wasn't, "all there." But, I loved it, even at night when I couldn't read it. It tickled me just to know it was there. When a picture or poem got too wrinkled and spotty from the dampness she just pasted another on top, so the inside of the outhouse eventually became a hodgepodge collage of art that appealed to her. Only "The Cremation" remained. When it became almost unreadable she wrote up another copy and pasted it up.

Another thing that pleased me was that it was a two-holer, with one of the holes being child-sized. I never liked those big holes with all the dark below.

The two bedrooms were small, one upstairs reached by a narrow stairwell, one down off the living room. The kitchen and pantry were miracles of planning. Shelves lined the walls and hooks hung from the ceiling, all in use. Dried herbs hung next to the wood stove she used for cooking and heating. The cookstove was always there, even after Uncle Boyd had the place electrically wired, and a small refrigerator put in. She admitted that the electric lights were better for the close needle work that she did, and electric heat in the winter was convenient on cold nights, but she never gave up the morning warmth and comfort of a wood fire. There was a small, stone fireplace in the living room, and I now believe that is the main reason she loved the house so.

The fireplace, and the little bedroom upstairs. It was Uncle Boyd's room. There was a high, four-poster bed, and mirrored chest of drawers. His fishing gear and hunting and camping clothes hung on nails behind the door. A mounted deer's head stared at us from the wall. I guess it was his, always kinda spooked us kids. But other than that the room looked more like a child's room than a mans.

An elaborate electric train could be set up on the floor from the box in the closet. A slingshot hung on a peg on the wall. Toy trucks and cars sat on the windowsill and shelves. Intricate puzzles and tinker toys, blocks and books filled the bookcase built along the wall under the sloping roof. There were also dolls with complete wardrobes made by Aunt Sophie, but the feel was essentially a boy's room.

Whenever a child stayed with her, and we did as often as possible, the room was ours. The room had a familiar warmth about it, not only because I spent so many nights playing and sleeping there, but because it was always the same.

My favorite thing in the room was the quilt on the four-poster. A simple tied quilt with bright colored squares, the design fascinated me, and the other cousins, for it was embroidered every which way with names. The whole family was there, all the aunts, uncles, cousins, and grandparents. I was up near the top so that my name was raised by the pillow when the bed was made up.

When bored I'd read the names and take comfort in being surrounded by all the people I loved, and even some I didn't but who were never the less of my blood. There was a mystery contained in the quilt. The names in the center, below "Sophie Elm" did not belong to "us": 'David Smithers', 'Amy Smithers', and, in bright blue, 'J. Sampson Smithers' and 'Lily Smithers'. The first time the oddness of it struck me I was about eight or nine. I puzzled over the names, trying to fit them to some relative seldom heard of or some long dead ancestor, but finally had to take the mystery to my Aunt to solve.

She was no help, only making me more curious. "Oh, those are some people I used to know a long time ago who I was very fond of. They don't mean anything to you." After much nagging through the years I got no further than a promise that maybe some day she would tell me about them, but she'd always deflect penetrating questions.

"Just look at your hands!" I curled them tightly into my brown palms. "Aren't you ashamed to have such dirty fingernails?" I was. One of the penalties of staying with Aunt Sophie was having to adhere to her standards of how neat a little girl should be. Clean and neatly rounded fingernails, clean and untangled hair, which meant tight braids, or, if I was lucky, and she had the time, ringlets. And every night without fail, visiting children suffered a maddening tickling lying flat on our backs in bed while she squeezed a dropper of chilly fluid into our noses.

"Stop squirming, and be quiet,' she would demand. "It's no skin off my back if you catch cold, but as long as you're with me you can at least try to help yourself!" She swore the drops kept us from catching colds. I don't know what her medical information was but we tried not to sneeze or drip when we were with her. The only relief from this maternal torture was reaching the magic age of thirteen.

"Now that you're thirteen you should be able to take care of yourself," she stated, when, a few days after my birthday I laid, apprehensive, beside my ten-year-old cousin Teri as she suffered the drops. Finished with Teri she handed me the bottle, completing the sentence, "at least as far as drippy noses is concerned," and left the room. I knew I was supposed to put the dang drops in my own nose, but, grinning at Teri I just set the bottle on the bed table.

"More for you." I said.

Now I was 22 and had forgotten the mystery of the names, but upon her first statement of, "David was mine," I remembered.

The blackberries were finally put up and stored on the pantry shelves. Aunt Sophie took a nap in her back bedroom and I went upstairs to rest on the bed. As always I checked my name first, 'Annie Elm'. It was now quite worn as were most of the cousins names, from our eternal running of our fingers over them, but the 'David,' 'Amy,' 'J. Sampson' and 'Lily Smithers' were scarcely touched. I felt of them now, tracing the letters gently in some wonder, as if meeting new, but old, friends for the first time. The quilt held less mystery, but more warmth than ever.

J. Sampson was still an unknown, but he was definitely kin to me.

Aunt Sophie stopped talking only when we were done with the day's work on the blackberries. The kitchen smelled sweet, the counters sticky from berry juice and sugar, the room hot and damp from our work and all the boiling of water and berries.

"We've earned a rest, my girl!" she said, wiping her forehead with the bottom of her apron before taking it off. She was finally as tired as me, I was relieved to go upstairs and open the window to let the little breeze of the late afternoon into the room.

As I laid the thin quilt aside to nap on the sheets in the hot room, I didn't think of a gray-haired Aunt Sophie downstairs tired from a hard day's work, but a young, black-haired, perhaps even lusty (the thought was still difficult to admit) Sophie, as young as myself, and obviously not so innocent as I'd always thought.

After our naps the evening cooled off enough that I brought in a few pieces of wood and stacked them by the fireplace. We ate tomato sandwiches with pieces of cheese and apple, drinking buttermilk in front of a small fire, 'cause she knew I liked it, not for need of warmth. After dinner she got out an afghan she was knitting, and with very little prodding, she picked up her story again.

17. Their Room, My Room

The whole lower floor was one big living room. The large fireplace was the first thing I saw clearly, almost as clearly as I saw David coming from it to me. Amy's hand dropped from my back; I was alone.

David's face at that moment is as clear to me now as if I had taken a photograph. His eyes were especially bright, his face was flushed from the fire, his hair slightly dark and wet with comb marks. His usual grin was absent, his sweet mouth slightly open like he'd been breathing deeply. I must of looked as frightened as I felt because his expression changed as he reached for me, his forehead wrinkled and his mouth tightened at the corners.

As aware as I was of David, I was even more aware of Amy, she was a blur of movement. While I stood frozen by the door and David moved in slow-motion towards me, Amy was busy to an extreme.

She'd thrown her coat onto a peg behind the door and I heard pans being banged around and dinner being made. Now faced with David I wanted to flee to the safety of Amy and 'women's work', but stood rooted to the spot.

Almost without me being aware of it David reached me and gently, hugged me. He would have kissed me right on the mouth but I squirmed away so he only brushed my cheek. Amy was right in the same room! I tried to cover my embarrassment with movement, like Amy was doing. I struggled to get out of my coat, David helped me, then hung my coat up beside his and Amy's. We stood still for an long time and even the kitchen area was quiet. I saw Amy looking at us, her face without expression. She caught my glance and once again she was full of purpose, her eyes focused on her husband.

"David! Take Sophie to the fire. She must be cold." It broke the spell.

"I was just going to! Sophie! You must be cold!"

"Well, I'm just a little chilly," I admitted. In truth, a cold fear shook my very heart.

David walked with his arm easily around my shoulders and sat me in his chair by the fireplace, pulling up a stool for himself. He no sooner sat down than he was up again, poking at the fire, adding another small log from a hole in the right side of the fireplace.

"What a beautiful fireplace. I like this room." I talked on about the room until David regained his composure. He and Amy filled the evening with stories of how they'd found this area, selected the place, built the house, how happy they were with it but their were improvements they wanted to add. Amy brought coffee and fried ham sandwiches which we ate at a table set close to the big window. It faced the sea, the view being the same as mine but more so, including my cabin. Every time either of them stopped talking I asked another question about something in the room, a piece of furniture, the house plants, a pretty or interesting picture on the wall. I wanted to listen to them talk all night. The thought of what lay ahead petrified me.

After what seemed like hours the talk ran out. We sat at the table in the stillness, with only a slight popping from the fire and an occasional hiss as a rain drop fell through the chimney into the flames. We could hear the ocean but the sounds within the room were most noticeable. I wanted to run out the door and down the path and into my cabin and lock the door.

Instead, I sat, waiting.

Amy breathed a deep sigh, which was loud in the quiet room.

"Well," she said, standing up. Her movement startled me. "Might as well do the dishes."

"I'll help." I said. My voice sounded strange. I picked up my dish to start clearing off and lurched up to help her, relieved to end the stillness, to have something to do that would further prolong the, I now know, inevitable step. But that wasn't her intent.

"No." She took the plate from my hand. "David, take Sophie to her," she corrected herself, "to your room. She's tired and needs to sleep."

He was beside me. Amy was right. At that moment I wanted nothing more than to be in bed, away from her, however normal she was trying to make this all seem. I wanted to escape. Firstmost in my mind were her words just before we had come in, that David was, "yours." Did she mean it? What was going to happen now?

Though it was David's idea and my final compliance that had got us into this situation, it was Amy who had managed this step to get me into the house. She'd helped smooth the evening with almost normal talk. David now needed to regain control, and so he did.

"Sophie, the staircase is right over there. The, uh, your room is to the right. I'll be up in a few minutes." I took my bag from beside the door and David led me to the steps which he didn't need to do as they were right in plain sight. I'd been aware of them all evening.

He said again, "I'll be right up." As I started up he called, "Be careful, the steps are steep." I didn't need that advice, either. In my heavy and frightened condition all I could do was lug myself slowly and carefully up the steps. There were firm rails on either side which helped some but it wasn't necessary. Before I was ready for it I was at the top. Their room was at the left, over the living room; my room was to the right, over the kitchen. So long as I lived there I never stopped thinking of them as 'their' room and 'my' room.

I no sooner got to my room and set my bag on the bed than I realized that I hadn't gone to the bathroom. It had been a nagging fullness all evening, I'd ignored it. I wasn't going to make it through the night. I looked under the bed. No chamber pot. Lord! I wanted to stay in the room but I had to go! I left my bag on the floor by the bed and headed back for the stairs. I wasn't trying to be sneaky, I was concentrating on being careful as I came down the stairs. I got to the bottom with so little noise that they didn't notice me. They were by the sink, his arms around her in a loving embrace. She was kissing his face, murmuring, "I know. It's ok. I love you, too."

I felt sick. The jealousy I'd kept submerged all evening (along with my bladder ache) surged through me and I rushed through the room for the door.

"Sophie! What's ...?" I heard David call. I mumbled something about the outhouse and was out before they could stop me. It was cold and raining which calmed the nausea I'd felt. I stumbled through the salal around the house making some noise that woke the chickens in the coop to the back of the house. Their squawking startled me until I could laugh and relax enough to search out the wooden walk running to the outhouse in the back. While in there I considered just heading back to my cabin and Punkin Sue Tiger. But I'd just have to go through all this again, unless I ran away. Where would I go? There was nothing to do but go back. I stopped by the coop and whispered to the chickens until I got my courage up to go back into the house. It felt odd just opening the door so I knocked lightly before going in.

Amy had finished the dishes and was sweeping up. The house was clean already, it was just busy work. Now that the moment was at hand she had nothing more to say. David was nowhere in sight. I went straight to the stairs, not having much to say myself. I forced myself to say, "Good night."

Her, "Nite," was short and almost curt. No doubt she didn't appreciate me breaking up her last moment with David, however accidentally.

When I got to my room I found David. He'd lit the lantern on the bedside table and was already in bed. I pushed the door shut. He watched me undress and put on my nightgown and smiled as I tugged it over my big tummy. I'd made one 'specially big for my condition but before long I had given it up and made a bigger one. I was glad to blow out the light but shy about getting into bed with David. He pulled back the covers and moved over to make room. If I was an artist like David I could still draw that scene my memory is so clear with it. Once in, he snuggled close to me. I finally relaxed and turned to him. We kissed for a long time, but didn't make love. I could never have relaxed enough for that on my first night in their house.

I'd heard Amy come up the stairs and cross the hall into their room - I'd held my breath. It was not possible for me to relax enough

… it just wouldn't have felt right.

He played with moving the baby around by pressing down easy on the little foot that poked up on my tummy, which made the baby shift inside me. We giggled and he did it again until I made him stop, I was afraid he might hurt the baby somehow even though his hands were so very gentle.

His love for me and the safety I felt in that bed, that first night and every night thereafter, completely overwhelmed me. I cried quiet tears and he comforted me, his hand stroking my skin in a way he never had before. Protective.

I felt safe with him. David went to sleep long before I did. I lay there feeling him close to me, listening to the night sounds of surf and the rain on the roof. I finally fell asleep.

18. Let Me Serve You..

I woke in the near dawn to David smoothing the blanket over me. He was already out of bed, leaning down, when he saw my eyes on him. He kissed me and whispered, "I must fix the fire. Go back to sleep. Come down when you're ready." I knew he was going to spend some time with Amy before I showed up downstairs, but, somehow, it didn't worry me.

The daylight of early morning woke me. My spot in the bed was warm. I put my hand over to where David had been, it was cool. I could feel the chill of the room on my face. I snuggled the covers up close around my neck - I didn't want to get up. Besides, I was scared again.

Nature's call forced me to leave the room, or I might be there still! The morning was easier than the night had been. The coolness that Amy had showed the night before was gone. She was easy with me, no hint that we'd spend the night any different from usual.

She sat at the table with piles of paper spread in front of her. Her hair was loosed from the bun of the night before, now caught up into a soft braid tied with a brown ribbon. She smiled at me as I came from the stairs across to her, said, "Good morning, dear," and moved her hand to invite me to sit down at the table with her.

"Not yet." I smiled back at her, it was impossible not to, and said, "I'll be right back," and, grateful for a normal reason to not stop and chat, I went out into a beautiful morning. The ground wasn't dry but the sky was, for which I thanked the gods. I breathed in probably the first comfortable breath I'd taken in weeks, and took the side walk to the house out back.

After I'd taken care of nature I walked around the ground for a few minutes, looking at the bushes and stumpy trees, just getting comfortable with being there. The chickens were already out of the coop, David must have been here. Maybe Amy took care of the chickens? It was something I could help with. I peeked in to look at the nests for eggs. The nests were at the back, not enough light for me to see whether they held eggs or not. I'd have gone in but a rooster left the group of hens and flew at me, screeching and threatening. Whoa! I backed up, not ready to challenge him! I'd not taken a wrap so when the frosty air began to sink in I gathered my courage and went back into the house.

"David's in the gable, painting," Amy said, indicating again a place at the table for me to sit.

The room was warm from coals in the fireplace. I picked up a piece of wood from the box by the hearth and put it on the fire. Puttering around.

"It's really cold this morning," I said.

She could hear the fear in my voice. Less than the night before, but still there. She rose from the table.

"Are you hungry?" she asked. She went to the sideboard and pulled a loaf of bread from the box there, and began slicing.

"I am," I said, "a little."

"No wonder," She opened the oven door, putting the putting the bread on the rack. She put a couple of pieces of wood in the stove firebox. The smell of toast filled the room.

"There's oatmeal here on the stove, and bowls up here," she indicated a shelf above and to the side of the stove while she went to the foot of the stairs. There was a narrow pull rope there that I hadn't noticed the night before, she pulled it sounding a bell way above us.

"David. In the gable. I know he'll want to eat something, and see that you are ok." I had the grace to blush. She had the grace to pretend she didn't notice. We could hear David coming down the stairs, she remarked on how pretty the frosty morning was and I said I thought so too. David was a relief, turning the corner at the bottom of the stairs and coming across the room to the kitchen table. He hesitated, this was new to him too, and then brushed his hand over my hair, a loving gesture that calmed me down.

He pulled out my chair and said, "Let me serve you, my lovelies." He filled three bowls with mush, put out spoons for us each, and sat down. Sophie had already brought the toast to the table where I'd buttered it, thankful for the work. I pushed the toast plate to the center of the table while she sat down, handing us each a napkin.

I started to reach for my oatmeal. "David," Amy said.

His head was already bowed. "Thank you, Lord. Amen." He lifted his head, smiled a big smile at both of us, and began spooning sugar on his oatmeal. We all three relaxed.

It was our first meal together, the first of many. We fell into a pattern that lasted for most of my time there: I prepared breakfast (for which I always set an attractive table, if I do say so myself). David fixed lunch, and, while I took a late afternoon nap, Amy cooked dinner. The other chores got done easily. David helped where needed and sometimes when not needed. Amy confided to me once when he was gone on his morning beach walk that he'd seldom helped around the house before, other than wood chopping and fixing things. The only reason we could come up with was that when we worked and he sat, there was too much suggestion of a harem serving their lord, and David certainly didn't want that. At least he said he didn't.

I loved the chicken coop that David had built. It looked more like a real house, but small, than the big one did. It became part of my mornings to collect the eggs. It soothed me to walk among them listening to their soft cheeps and clucks as they pecked after bugs on the ground, or grabbed at the corn I threw out for them. After a few days the hens let me enter the coop without fuss and take their prizes. The rooster was crazy, never accepted me, but I flapped my arms back at him and screeched louder than him and he backed off enough for me to get into the coop. It would crow at odd hours of the night and couldn't be depended on as an alarm clock unless you wanted to get up at 2:00, 3:00, or 4:00 a.m. By dawn it was often asleep, too tired from crowing through the night to greet the morning!

That first day went quickly with learning where things were and house cleaning. My initial impression of Amy as a homemaker was that she was a spotless housekeeper because we cleaned all day! The cupboards, shelves, bedrooms, floor - we washed down, straightened, and swept. She wouldn't allow me to do the heavy work so David asked me to take a walk on the beach with him. I thought that Amy would like to have the house to herself for awhile. We left.

He helped me down the slippery path, and as we passed my cabin I heard Punkin Sue Tiger yowl from inside. I'd forgotten all about him! When I opened the door he ran out and raced around my feet, then around David's, crying loudly the whole time, both mad and glad I suppose. He ran off to the bushes.

"We can pick him up when we come back," David said, laughing, and I agreed with him. I was so in love with him that at that moment whatever he said, went. And then, I wanted to get down to the beach too.

Once there he put his arm around my waist and we walked close, our hips bumping. I began to feel my insides and bones softening, the first time since Amy's appearance at my door. The wind was bitterly cold, biting into my face and hands. David suggested we go back.

"Not just yet, please." I pulled him to a sheltered place below the cliff. In the privacy of a deserted beach I put my arms around him and hugged him close. Comforted, we sat on a damp log. There, with winds that dissolved our voices beyond a couple of feet, I questioned him.

"What does Amy think of your great plan now?"

For not the first time, and certainly not the last, David was exasperated with me.

"I don't know why you continue to question her! Amy is as you see her! She has no secret dislike of you that she's hiding! She likes you! Of course," I knew it, he was about to admit that all was not rosy between them, her act was all a farce. "She is worried about you working too hard, and wonders whether you'll miss having your family around when the baby comes. And she says you should have a doctor here when you deliver."

She was worried about me! Not about her and David. Of course she'd probably keep that to herself, but.... My suspicion of her, most active when I was away from her, lessened.

David's hand was resting absentmindedly on my swollen lap. Suddenly the baby kicked and his hand flew off as if burnt. "Whoa! Who's in there? A tiger?" He bent close to the mound and began talking to our baby. "Who are you in there? How's the weather, huh? Warmer than out here for sure! Be glad you've got such a nice nest. Soon you'll be out here playing on the beach with us. I'll show you how to build a sand castle and you can tell me what it was like in there. I've forgotten. What are you? That kick was a boy's kick. But maybe you're a strong girl like your mommy. Just wait till you meet your mommy! She's a funny lady, always asking questions when she should be quiet and being quiet when she should be asking questions."

He looked up at me and stroked the baby through my clothes. "Your mommy is beautiful, too." His eyes were so tender and thoughtful I reached out and pulled him to me. I thought no more of Amy and what he'd said until a few days later.

But his mention of a tiger recalled me to a start, Punkin Sue Tiger! Cold in the bushes! We left the cold beach and rescued our unhappy cat. He settled into the new house like he'd always been there, part of the family.

That night I went to bed right after supper. The time after dinner was always easier for me on the nights he spent with her because it seemed, it was, more natural to me. I loved sleeping with him but never got used to it when she was in the next room.

19. The Rooster Crowed at Dawn

The days flowed one into another. After I'd been there for about two weeks Amy brought up the subject of a doctor. I refused to consider it.

She pleaded, "If anything goes wrong I'll never forgive myself. Maybe if I'd had a doctor with my baby everything would have been all right." She saw the struck look on David's face. "But maybe not. We'd planned to but I thought I had plenty of time. Some things just aren't meant to be, I guess. And look! We're going to have a baby anyway, even if it's not just as we thought it'd be."

I was embarrassed, but she didn't seem to be. That was her way. She accepted what was, not the way things were 'supposed' to be. I've always been at war with the facts, trying to turn things into something I can make sense of. I was used to things being natural and simple, and having a doctor didn't seem natural to me. They'd got me into their house, made me a part of their family so that I almost felt comfortable there, but on the subject of bringing in a stranger to help me in what I saw as a simple affair, I could not be budged. I was going to birth a child and wasn't married to the father, not even a doctor was going to know that. There would be no doctor.

In my last two months I was glad I wasn't alone. The cabin had been so desperately lonely and now I was, in spite of myself, happy. David and Amy laughed a lot, talking and teasing each other with old stories of funny things that had happened to them. While we popped corn over the fire in the long-handled popper we discussed the strange, unexplained, spooky things that raise the hairs on the back of your neck. On really stormy nights Amy would sit on the braided rug by the fireplace and play the flute. Sometimes David would sing softly and with very little coaxing I would join him. In my eighth month when the baby was seeming to be trying to kick his way out, we found that if Amy played soft and close to me the baby quieted down. He enjoyed the music too. The only one who wanted out of that was Punkin Sue Tiger. He'd either go sit by the door and meow to go out, or go up the stairs and I'd find him sleeping in the corner of my room. He was not a musical cat.

As my time neared I stayed around the house more. My heartburn was miserable and my stomach muscles started practicing for birth. It alarmed Amy and David more than me because I'd seen it happen with Amanda's four births. It did spur me to a flurry of sewing and crocheting. Punkin Sue Tiger gave me fits with the thread!

David went into town and bought yards and yards of white flannel which Amy and I made into nightgowns and diapers. I embroidered the nightgowns with blue forget-me-nots and yellow daisies and we made a flannel-backed quilt from my scrap bag. David stopped painting for a while to finish a cradle. The wood was still there from when Amy was pregnant. He'd put it away when she lost the baby. Now he hummed to himself as he sanded and polished and carved. I sewed. While we worked Amy put away her sewing to play her music. It was all more natural than I could have believed.

Preparing for a baby should be the happiest thing humans do and for us, it was. We were all excited but they were a little afraid, too. Neither of them had been around at the birth of a baby. David had been the youngest in his family and Amy's younger brother and sister had seemed to just be there with no notice.

I was afraid of the pain. Amanda had carried on so with the births of her four that I determined not to scream if I could help it. I also knew that Amanda was more dramatic than me, and angry at her husband for not being there made everyone, including herself, suffer. When he would come home, after the birth, she would give him a blow by blow description of her suffering and swear never to go through it again. She wouldn't stop until he begged her to forgive him, and comforted her, promising never to be away again. But once she had the new baby in her arms she forgave and forgot and was happy the next time she was carrying another child. After I went back to them I shamed him into staying with her through the births and she was much calmer.

My last week was the worst. March going out with a roar. The ocean stormed and the clouds poured the last heavy winter rains on us. On April 3rd the sea calmed down and the rain lessened to a drizzle and I felt more energetic than I had in days. I baked enough bread and rolls to last a week, then mopped the floor and finally stopped, only because Amy was worried. I went to bed early because she insisted, and once she got me to stop I wanted to do nothing but rest. I wasn't physically tired, just wanted to be alone for a while. It was Amy's night with David. I could hear their voices from downstairs, until her flute lulled me to sleep.

Early in the night I awoke. All was quiet, then I heard that crazy rooster crow and, figuring that was what had wakened me, I tried to get comfortable again to go back to sleep. A sharp tightening at the bottom of my belly brought me to attention. This felt different than the other cramps, deeper, more insistent. It passed and I lay waiting in the dark, alert. After an eternity it grabbed again. I kept quiet, not yet ready to share this with anyone. I was excited but protective of this miracle that was happening between my baby and me. I thought about the baby and prayed that all would go well. The pains got harder, closer together and I didn't want to be alone any longer. I called out softly, "David." I no sooner said his name that he was in the room with me.

"Sophie! What's the matter? Is it the baby? Is it time?" His words tumbled in a rush of excitement and fear. He lit my lamp, took one look at me and shouted, "Amy!"

She must have been waiting for his call she was there so quick. She took my hand as a contraction grabbed me, I squashed her hand in mine. She took charge.

"David, start the fire in our bedroom. Put clean sheets on the bed. We'll move her in there where it's warmer, and, we need some hot water to wash with."

While David hurried around getting everything ready Amy sat with me, talking softly and holding my hand. When their room was ready she helped me from the bed and warm water suddenly rolled down my legs. My bag of waters had broken and I knew the birth was not far away.

Walking was difficult. It had been hard to get up, now it was hard to get down into a bed again. David helped us into their room, then Amy sent him downstairs to heat up more water and to scout out the old flannel sheets she'd put aside for this. She helped me into the bed.

"Well, Amy, this is it." I tried to joke between pains. "I hope you're ready. No more peace and quiet in this house."

She gave me her hands to pull on as a big wave of pain grabbed me. "Ready or not, this is it! We'll handle whatever comes. You just relax, and push!"

Yes, indeed - easier said than done!

I didn't need any urging to push. My body was fixed on it. She let go my hands and gave me a towel tied to the head of the bedstead to pull on. David came into the room. His lips were tight around his mouth. He hovered over me.

"Ok?" he asked, "Are you ok?"

I nodded. Despite myself I groaned and David grabbed my hand that was stretched out to him. I wasn't aware of anything other than trying to push the pain away. I wasn't thinking of the baby, just doing what my body demanded. When I got my breath I noticed the heat in the room - David had built quite a fire! "David, please, open the window."

"It's cold out there," he protested.

"Well, it's hot in here!" I said, "Please." He went to the window and opened it a crack, that small coolness from the sea relaxed me until the next pain came. Another few minutes that seemed to go on forever until a final crushing squeeze in my back, belly and bottom and I felt the baby start to come out. One more push, it was over and the pain stopped. I was so glad! David immediately shut the window.

Amy grabbed a flannel and with the stopping of the pain I focused on her. She scooped the baby up into the cloth as easy as if she'd always done it. His wail filled the room. My baby's face wasn't the only one with tears. Wetness streamed down Amy's face, and

David's. "For heavens' sake," I demanded, my own voice none too steady, "Is it a boy, or a girl?"

"He's a little Sampson," Amy laughed through her tears, "A head full of hair and all." She handed him over to David who put him on my flat belly. He brushed at his face with the back of his hand, and turned to help Amy. I paid no attention to the delivery of the afterbirth or the cutting of the cord. I combed his wet hair with my fingers, it was a black mass that went down to his neck!

We named him Jonathan Sampson but always called him Sampson, except when he was naughty, then he was Jonathan Sampson Smithers!

I had thought I was grown up and understood life but it took Sam's birth to see the full range of it. As I lay there stroking his so, so soft, perfect little body I realized that he would die someday. I wanted to protect him from that and had to accept that as I had not been able to prevent his birth, I could also not stop his death. But I swore I'd try to make his life pleasant and worthwhile, that I'd love him forever.

Light came through the window, along with the noise of the morning surf. That crazy rooster was just below the window and damned if he didn't crow at the dawn! For once he was on time and had something to crow about! He brought my thoughts back from death to life. We all grinned like we'd done something special.

The rain stopped and the early sun turned the room a rosy pink. Amy moved around cleaning up while David put some more wood on the fire. Jonathan lay quietly beside me, looking up at me. His little face was so cute to watch. His forehead wrinkled and his mouth opened and shut. Such a tiny nose! "Would you like some toast and egg?" Amy asked me. She smoothed the blanket at the bottom of the bed, ready to leave the room. Her eyes glowed with a soft happiness. She was happy for me, and satisfied at the birth of our baby.

Little Sammy started at her voice, his head moving against my breast to find his breakfast, too. I loved that movement and never tired of it. "Yes!" I said, "Me too. This Sampson baby is gonna eat. We're starved!" She nodded and left the room to start the day's work.

David took his Bible from the top of the chest and sat down in the chair beside the bed. He looked at Sam and me, nodding as he opened the Bible to the front. Below,

Married: Amy Johnston and David Smithers,

           July 18, 1907

he wrote,

Born to Sophie Adele Elm and David Andrew Smithers:

     Jonathan Sampson Smithers,

     April 4, 1919. May God bless.

20. Love of Work

Amy made me stay abed for a week. She wanted me to stay down at least two weeks but I wouldn't hear of it. I was restless to be up and about, sure that she was going to wear herself out running up and down the stairs bringing my meals. David was in the room with every little whimper from Samson. I had plenty of milk and David delighted in watching me feed the baby.

"Lucky boy, Sampson," he teased as the milk began to drip from my breasts whenever the baby cried to be fed. David would lift Samson from his cradle (if he wasn't already holding him!) and little Sampson's mouth would search for the milk, nuzzling into his chest. He'd lay Sam beside me and watch with a grin as Samson clamped greedily on a nipple and begin sucking with a fierce labor, his body softening as the milk flowed from my body to his. I enjoyed it as much as they did because my breasts were swollen with the milk and only Sampson could relieve it. We would both relax after he ate. David would burp him and put him back in my arms. Often I would waken, not knowing I had gone to sleep. David would be gone, and Sampson would be sleeping in his cradle, making his little snorty noises that were so sweet.

It was all very peaceful and enjoyable to rest and be waited on, but after the week I decided it was enough, time to get back to my own room and into our regular routine. They protested but I insisted so we changed beds and bedrooms again. Sampson stayed in their room because it was warmer (we all said) and bigger, (we all said, but we all really knew that as hungry as I was for this baby, Amy needed him. I wondered, later, of course, if that had been the best for me, but, that was later).

If Sampson woke at night to be fed David brought him to me. David slept for a week with me, mostly at Amy's urging, then we went back to every other night. Days, David took the cradle downstairs and we all gave Sampson so much attention that he seldom had a reason to cry.

Evenings I remember especially. He'd often whimper a little from gas or something; I'd lay him across my knees and rub his back and stroke his sides while Amy played her flute. It never failed to quiet him. His bright, big blue eyes would turn toward her and he'd kick his arms and legs and gurgle almost as if he was trying to march and sing in time with the music.

When he was just little he could lay across my lap, then he grew enough to lay facing me lengthwise with my legs close together. I'd bring my knees up and play with his hands and tickle his belly. He especially liked the 'bee game', we'd all burst into giggles with him when I finished with my circling finger that ended with the funny buzz into his tummy or under his arm, or under his chin.

David returned to his painting and made one of me nursing the baby. He made me more beautiful than I was, with my hair falling loosely around my shoulders, and caught Sampson's serious look of concentration, the furrowed forehead that the baby had when he was working at dinner. He titled it "Love of Work" and though it was his best he would not sell it. Most of his paintings that Spring were a record of life within our house.

Amy returned to her writing and did a series of poems and short stories, some of them springing from the same well as David's drawings - Sampson. The poems concentrated on the wonder of birth but the stories were tales of a small boy named Sampson, and his adventures at his seaside home. They were wild fantasies of him taming sea lions and a whale and riding over the waves on the backs of seagulls that came whenever he called. He had only to play his flute and all sorts of creatures came to play with him, a miniature Tarzan of the sea.

In late July, when Sampson was almost three months old she began reluctantly to pack David's paintings and her writing to go on her annual trip to the city. She didn't want to go and worried that she was leaving us with no one to care for us. We just laughed and reassured her that we would be ok and to enjoy her vacation.

"Vacation!" she sputtered. "You two better hope I bring home plenty of money from my 'vacation'!" She finally left but agreed on to be gone for only a month, even that was more than she could bear, she said, but what must be done, must be done.

I was surprised at how much I missed her in the house. We'd grown close and I loved her, but still I was looking forward to having David and the baby all to myself for a month. But the house seemed almost empty without her laughter and singing as we worked together or played with Samson. He missed her too and when we sat by the fire at night he would look bewildered when he whimpered and there was no Amy to play for him. I think David missed her least of all because he was used to her yearly absence and for once he had other people to talk to. It was now clear why he'd been so happy to have me when Amy was gone before. David hated being alone. The only difference that we both enjoyed from her departure was that we made love almost every night, but in my bed, not theirs.

She came back in early August, radiant. She burst into the house with David close behind staggering under the load of her luggage. She'd gone with one trunk and the paintings and come back minus the paintings but with two trunks! Her brown eyes were dancing when she flew across the room and threw her arms around me. Her hug almost squeezed the breath out of me.

"I sold all of David's work the first week!" She bubbled with happiness, lifting Samson off the rug where he was laughing and trying to talk to her. "You little love!" She kissed him and held him out to admire him and pulled him close for another big hug. "You've grown so much! Auntie Amy missed you so much!" Another squeeze, he squealed, she calmed down and told us, "I spent the next week with a publisher and 'The Mother's Journal' bought all my poems and 'Springtime Books' offered me a contract to publish all my Sampson stories in individual books, the first to come out next winter!"

To say we were all happy to be together again and to have such good fortune to celebrate is to understate it! David killed a fat hen in celebration and we had chicken and dumplings, David's favorite, with fresh lettuce and tomatoes from our garden, with blackberry pie for dessert. The new trunk sat by the door where David had dropped it when he drug it in. It was heavy.

The house was a home again as we sat together at the table over coffee, Sampson asleep in his almost too small cradle by the fireplace. Amy was still bubbling and I wondered why. David and I were happy to have her back but we were puzzled at how she continued to laugh and finally as the late summer sun began to set she burst out, she had secrets in the trunk.

"Well! You two! I have still another surprise! Bigger news even than the books and paintings!" She jumped up from the table and went to the new trunk. She fiddled with the catch, got it open and reached in. She had presents for us all. A lovely dress of a deep rose color, and a beautiful pearl necklace, for me. She helped me get the clasp fastened. I loved the feel of the pearls on my throat.

For David there were new pants, a shirt, a gold watch chain, and a cunning pocket watch that chimed off the hours. He wound it and then was immediately impatient for the hour to pass.

For Sampson a toy train that David wound up and watched it run in circles on a small track. A small stuffed whale, that the baby grabbed onto, tasted, and held the softness against his cheek. Clothes enough to last until he was a bigger boy.

For herself Amy had a new, rich dark blue, wool coat and hat to match. She shrugged into the coat, set the hat on at a sassy angle and paraded around the room while we admired her. A light blue dress in the latest fashion, but no prettier than mine. And yards and yards of material. Satins, velvets, woolens, and lots of flannel.

"What's with all the flannel?" David wondered aloud.

She threw her arms around him and then quieted down so I barely heard her say, "That's for nightgowns and bedding for our baby."

"Samson has all he needs," he started to say, but she put her fingers against his lips to shush him.

"The new baby. Our baby."

After all the years of waiting David's cup of babies was overflowing.

"Oh, Amy," was all he could say. I got up and kissed them each on their foreheads and went to bed.

I lay sleepless listening to smothered giggling and finally the soft notes of Amy's flute drifting upstairs. What would this mean to me, and Sampson? Would Sampson be shoved aside? Would they love their baby more than him? I couldn't imagine it but I knew the power of 'blood' enough to worry.

The next morning I learned that the last two weeks had been spent shopping, visiting friends, and seeing a doctor. She'd suspected she was pregnant when she left but said nothing for fear of another disappointment. It had really been the only reason she had gone, otherwise she would have sent David this time because she hadn't wanted to miss a whole month of Sampson's growing. And, she said, she had missed me too.

"I'll never leave here again for that long!" she declared, her jaw as set as the night she had led me up the hill. "From now on I'm a mother, and a writer," she said, "and David can be the salesman. Or get the buyers to come here." She was full of plans. "When the children are older we can all take the train to Utah and show them off to Grandma's and Grandpa's and aunts and uncles galore."

"What did the doctor say?" I asked her.

"That I'm perfectly healthy and as long as I'm careful I should have no trouble. And you can bet I will be! Just to be sure though I'm going to see a doctor here. He advised it. And David wants me to."

She was in her third month already which relieved some of our fear. Amy complained that we were treating her too delicately, watching her like a pot about to boil over. We tried to treat her condition as they had mine, with naturalness and joy, but there was no getting around our worrying over every little pain and stepping in to ease her way as we could. Despite her protests, Amy too, took care, moving slower and taking no chances. She would let Samson onto her lap but she didn't lift him there. She let him crawl up offering her hands for him to pull up on. Once there he snuggled easily into her. When he got restless she asked David or I to lift him off. But truly she didn't have to take too much care with that little baby boy, he sensed that she needed gentleness; around her he moved more slowly. His heart and senses were like his father, alert to his women. We all eased Auntie Amy's way as much as we could. For them it was a gentle winter and spring. For me, it was different.

21. A Hollow House

Sampson was crawling at six months, he had to be watched by someone all the time. If he was on his blanket on the floor he would crawl off to follow daddy. We learned to watch him. Daddy decided that if he wanted to go so much, it was time for an adventure. On a fall day that was warm and with only a bare breeze, we packed a basket and took him for his first picnic at the beach.

I hadn't allowed David to take him before. I was afraid he would get sunburned, or catch cold, or some terrible thing. Getting down to the beach by the path, with the baby and the basket to be carried, and a pregnant woman to maneuver, was a tricky job. The path was not slippery, but steep and with the slickness of dry sand.

Finally getting to the beach we went to a secluded place David and I knew about. The grass and salal were squashed flat. If Amy suspected why the area was so beat down she didn't mention it.

While David built a small fire to heat water for tea to go with our sandwiches Amy and I spread a blanket on the sand. I laid Sampson on it. He immediately flipped over to all fours and started scooting forward. Straight to the sand, and a mouthful. I cleaned him up while Amy laughed. My cleaning annoyed David.

"A little sand isn't going to hurt him. Let him enjoy himself. He'll stop when it doesn't taste good anymore." I pulled Samson back to the center of the blanket. I guess I was a little rough when brushed the sand from his mouth and hands and said, "Dirty boy! Shame!"

Both David and Amy were shocked. For the second time I saw David begin to be truly angry. The baby started to cry and David pulled him away from me. He soothed him, "It's OK. The sand is nice, isn't it?"

He soon had Sampson laughing again but the first crack was there.

The picnic didn't go well. David knocked Amy's cup of tea over onto the blanket. Our argument had made her nervous and she lashed out at him, "Don't be so clumsy, David. You're worse than the baby." He didn't answer, but got up and walked down the beach. In strained silence we watched him go over to Haystack Rock. The tide was far out that day so that most of the base was exposed. He poked around in the tide pools for about a half hour then returned. He looked refreshed but his eyes were still a dark blue, a sure sign that he was still upset. Food would perhaps restore his spirits. Amy and I stumbled over each other's words in our eagerness to soothe him.

"There's still a bacon sandwich," Amy offered, while I held out a boiled egg. "I'll peel it if you like?" He shook his head, catching his upper lip with his bottom teeth, a mannerism he had that annoyed me.

"Nah, I've had all I need." He reached over to Sampson and chucked him under his chin. Sampson wiggled over towards him. Speaking to Sampson, David said, "Hey, boy, I think the wind is coming up - what do you think?" Sampson grinned at him. Looking at Amy, David said, "We better go back to the house."

It was one of the few times that I felt left out, different, odd somehow. I didn't like it. I kept my fear inside me and didn't respond. I knew that Amy didn't want to go back, I could tell by the dismayed look on her face - she didn't get to come to the beach much since she had gotten bigger in the tummy. Sampson was having such a good time we all knew he was happy where he was. It was a beautiful day. But to argue with that set jaw would have been useless.

We packed the picnic gear back in the basket. Amy and I shook the blanket together and after folding it she hugged it close to her chest. She made a joke about it being easier back up the path since we were carrying the food inside us. I couldn't help grinning when David joked, "Yes, but you have a heavier load than we do!" and patted her tummy. He carried the basket, I carried Sampson, and Amy followed using the blanket as ballast.

Reaching the path David went up first and setting the basket on the grass he reached down and took Sampson from me. When I reached the top I took the baby and David turned to go back down to help Amy, but she was already halfway up the path. He sucked in his breath and, "Amy!" came out sharply.

She looked up, reached out a hand to have him pull her up. The motion threw her off balance, she slipped, sliding back down the path. From his reaction you would have thought she'd fallen from a thirty-foot cliff rather than just slipping a few feet into loose sand. They fussed over each other at the bottom of the path. I stood there holding a squirming Sampson. I was as concerned as they were but I couldn't do anything. I knew she couldn't be hurt by that little fall but I didn't know about the baby.

I called down, "Is Amy ok? Can I help?"

David mumbled something about, "Don't know," and paid no more attention to me.

Finally, feeling forgotten and tired of trying to hold Sampson I called down, "I'm going on up. I've got to put the baby down. I'll be back."

He looked up long enough for me to see the worry in his eyes. "No. That's ok. We'll be there soon."

The house sounded hollow, more so because I knew that David and Amy, though only a little ways away, were not with me at all. It was their problem and though we celebrated good times together and shared my worries, this worry was theirs alone and I was only at the edge.

I busied myself at washing up Sampson. He was cranky and tired and I was angry and didn't know why. With water that wasn't very warm I scrubbed his naked little body, then went after the sand in his ears. Sampson was as mad as I now. Scooping handfulls of water I splashed it into his ears and kept a firm hold around his slippery, fat little middle. He twisted away and got a face full of water, letting out a scream of pure mad. I yanked him from the basin and slapped him on his bare bottom. The crack! was loud in what I thought was an empty room. For a long second there was a silence after the noise, then the room filled with a deep, angry, "Sophie!" and a shocked, "Oh!" and the baby's howl poured over David and Amy's words.

Honestly, I was as horrified as they. I loved that little one more than my own life even, yet in a fit of despair I'd lashed out even quicker than I would have at one of Mandy's children. As bad as it was, and as I felt, I also was embarrassed that they had seen me hit the baby. I hadn't hurt him but he screamed as if I'd tried to throttle him.

Amy rushed over and tried, gently, saying, "Here, just let me take him," but I refused. I wrapped a towel around him and carried him past a white-lipped David to my bed upstairs where we both crawled under the covers and cried together. No one came up and soon the baby fell asleep. I was too ashamed to go downstairs. The heat of the day had made me sweaty, I was exhausted. Soon I slept too, Sampson's breath warm on my face.

It was almost dark when his soft pawing at my chest woke me. I gave him my breast, he latched on. The slurp was a peaceful happy sound and our sleep had erased our mutual anger. Full, he was easy to dress. His skin was cool from a breeze that came through the half-open window. I put him in a short cotton dress that left his legs free to crawl but covered his arms. the light blue lace at the neck and arms brought out the bright blue of his eyes, David's eyes. His face was pink with the sunset that shadowed the room. A surge of love for him and remorse for both of us swept through me and I hugged him close. His softness always amazed me. My happy boy giggled and his little hands grabbed onto my hair, and tugged. I pried his fingers open and finally had my head free. He laughed and reached for my hair but I was too quick for him.

"No, no, naughty little Sampson," I cooed while I nibbled at his chubby fingers. He shrieked with joy so I dropped him to the bed and attacked his cool toes.

"This little piggy went to market, this little piggy stayed home." I wiggled the sturdy middle toe. "This little piggy had roast beef, and this little piggy had none!" By the time I reached, "...piggy cried all the way home," he was almost convulsed with laughter and waving his feet so that the last little piggy-toe slipped from my grasp. I finished with kisses all over and bubbled my lips against his throat. He grabbed me around the neck and came up clinging to me. I wrapped one arm around him and with my free hand grabbed a shawl from the top of the dresser and folded it around his back and chilly feet. We were ready to go downstairs.

I knew what we looked like when we came into the living room, compared to the way we'd left. My hair was mussed in a way that I knew David liked. Both Sampson and I were pink from our play.

David was standing at the stove stirring a pot of beans. The room smelled good, and safe. Amy, at the fireplace, put a short log onto the fire and politely nodded at us then sat again in the padded rocker. The room with the small fire and warm food smell was very comfortable but the air was heavy with disapproval.

I felt I couldn't bear it if either of them mentioned the afternoon. For a moment my happiness slipped - cold fear in the pit of my stomach snapped through me and I determined to pretend nothing had happened. I blew again on Sampson's neck and he giggled, which caused Amy to put down the book she'd picked up, and look at us, or rather, at Sampson. She talked directly to the baby, "Oh, all happy now, huh?" He babbled at her and, forcing a laugh, I handed him to her.

"He wants his Auntie Amy." I talked to her through Sampson. "How are you, Aunt Amy?" I put Sampson in her now outstretched arms.

"Aunt Amy's just fine now." She took on the pretense, "Just a little tired."

"Well, then," I said brightly, "Mommy better help Daddy with dinner then," and turned before she could continue.

I crossed the room quickly and lightly, playfully, put my arm around David's shoulders and looked down into the pot. He didn't pull away from my touch but didn't lean in to me, either. My arm felt heavy. "Beans, huh!" My voice was forced but my fear drove me on.

He was close, but distant. "Almost done?" I asked, softer, but it seemed that my voice cracked in an empty room. "Looks like you used up the last of the pork,"

He mumbled, "Um huh." I ignored the briefness of his answer and acted as if we'd had a normal conversation, and a normal day.

"Well, I guess I got here just in time. How would you like some biscuits?"

A short, "OK," from the man I loved and who now was avoiding looking at me as much as I was avoiding looking at him.

"And a little salad?" I still had my arm on his shoulder.

"I'll go," he said, still distant but I saw and felt his body relax a little and the fear in my stomach loosened. He took the bucket from a nail on the wall by the door and left for the garden.

Making the quick biscuits gave me an armor against any but the lightest talk with Amy. That room that usually felt so spacious to me was now cramped, small.

I mixed and rolled and cut while chatting on about new clothes for Sampson. Amy fell in with it, no more eager than I to renew the unpleasantness of the afternoon.

When David came back he brought not only lettuce and tomatoes from the garden but new corn, a rare thing as the coast climate made it hard to grow. He was happier, lighter than when he'd left, perhaps because it was such a beautiful evening outside.

He put the corn on the table. It was already shucked, explaining why he'd been gone longer than necessary. I admired the small yellow ears while he put on a pan of water to boil. The thing I feared most was silence so I talked and talked, about the corn, the garden, the lovely night, the baby, until finally they were drawn into the happy atmosphere I was working so hard to create. By the time we sat down to the table for dinner, with only the lamp and the fire for light, the coldness in my stomach had eased. Amy ate with Sampson on her lap, feeding him a bit of mashed bean now and then to keep his hands out of her plate. David finally gave him a scraped-clean carrot to hold and nibble on.

"Sophie and I are going to make Sampson some new clothes," Amy said.

"New clothes!" David smiled, and my spirits soared at the sight. "He already has more clothes than I do!"

"Those are baby clothes! He's getting to be a little boy."

We were in such a hurry for him to grow up!

"His knees are red from crawling and I think a pair of pants would suit him just fine!"

"Pants!" David pretended to be shocked. "Why, I didn't wear long pants 'till I went to school!"

"David, this is 1919, not the 1880's!"

He started to protest but Amy cut him short. "We're going to cover his knees and that's that."

"Well," he said firmly, trying to maintain his control of things, ignoring our grins. "A big boy with long pants shouldn't be sitting on laps at the table." He reached over and tickled Sampson on his belly. "I'll begin your high chair tomorrow. How about that?"

Sampson arched his back and the carrot flew across the room. David got it, washed it, and handed it back to the baby, who promptly dropped it again. Sampson's game went on until David took him on his lap and held him until dinner was over.

The evening was quiet with Amy reading, me cleaning up and then sewing, and David trying to figure what he needed for the chair while Sampson lay rolling around his feet playing with a stuffed doll.

We went to bed early with me deciding to have the baby in with me. I was glad it wasn't my night with David. I opened the window that looked out upon the ocean, the air was glorious and warm, reminding me almost painfully of the night on the beach that now seemed so long ago, when being here was all new, and I'd not yet met David. I wanted time before we slept together again. I wanted to snuggle close and if he'd pulled away it would have sickened. Still, as always, I missed him and was grateful for the quiet snoring sound from Sampson's cradle close to my bed.

22. Merry Christmas

Life seemed to be again as it had been before the bad day but I noticed a strain in our easy- going feeling towards each other. I grew sharper with the baby as he started getting into things and it became more of a chore to keep him clean and unhurt. At seven months Sampson was walking around the furniture, pulling himself up on the bookcase and pulling things down. By early December, going into his eighth month we had to watch him all the time to keep him from crawling upstairs, or, if someone went outside, he would skoot for the open door.

I started to feel like I had to do everything. Amy was approaching her seventh month, and, by the doctor's orders, she rested a lot, downstairs. She watched Sampson and played with him when she wasn't sewing, or reading, or writing. The main job, of course, of taking care of him was mine. David spent hours painting in their room because the "coop" was too cold. If the weather was even halfway decent I went out, taking Sampson, or, braving the cold wind, with David.

We'd pass my old cabin, me feeling sorry for it being empty. I worried about the flowers. The rose bushes stayed hardy through the winter but they suffered from the wind, or so it seemed to me as the wind sculpted them to parallel the house. The next summer they bloomed with big, full roses proving that we don't always know what's best for flowers. Or for people.

Whether with David, or him and Sampson, when we got down to the sand I was always cheered. When I was right on it I loved the briny smell of the ocean and the noisy waves, but I only needed a little bit of it. I worried about Sampson getting cold, or I'd start to think about making the bread to go with the soup we most always had simmering - I'd want the warmth of the house and back we'd go!

When Sampson wasn't with us, David and I once in a while stopped at my old cabin on the way back, to build a fire to warm the cabin and stave off the coast mold. "Just keeping it up for Mrs. Hawley." There I'd let David have his way with me, or mine with him! as the cabin warmed and dried. I loved being alone there with him but as Amy's time grew closer so did our concern about leaving her for too long.

David enjoyed the winter, especially his first with two women and a small child to keep him company. I felt better than I had the previous winter, naturally, but there were more and more days of fog and rain which made me feel closed in. The last winter I'd hated because I'd been so terribly lonely, and afraid. This winter was much easier, but still, by Christmas I was restless and we still had at least two more months of coast winter, and Amy's birthing to get through.

For Christmas David killed another hen, and I braved the cold to walk to the store in town to buy a small ham. I made a rice pudding that Sampson loved, all over his face! And with carrots and apples we celebrated. Our gifts were few - it was our only Christmas together - I remember them well.

David wanted to eat breakfast before we opened our gifts that lay under the small tree he'd cut from the woods behind the house. Amy looked at me in pretend despair - it was barely dawn. She flung up her arms like she was giving up.

"If I live through a hundred and fifty Christmases with you, David Smithers, God forbid, I'll never understand...." She turned back to me, her eyes wide and eyebrows lifted. "I do understand him Sophie, I really do! He loves surprises, and he hates them." She paused, I urged her on.

"Explain it to me then, it is something to do with a man's stomach always coming first?"

"Here now, you two! Don't gang up on me. I just think a little something, maybe a little oatmeal to tide us over. You know we always...." He started toward the stove but Amy blocked his way, her belly making a good barrier.

126

"Yes, I know 'we always' but this time we don't! This time we open our presents first."

"But, why?"

"Because I say so," she answered, "and you know better than to annoy a pregnant woman!" She gave him a little shove that tumbled him into a chair.

"You see, Sophie," she addressed me again as if David wasn't there, "he hates it when it's all over. He waits so long. Christmas is his favorite day. He fumbles around the packages, feeling this one and that, doesn't matter if it's his or not. You saw him!"

I had. Just like a kid, down on his knees prowling around the tree, squeezing the presents.

Sampson didn't know the "rules", all he knew was pretty colors under, of all things, a big bush thing in the house. We all heard a ri-i-p! and, "Da Da," and saw Sampson waving a harmonica, then as with everything, straight to his mouth for a good chew. One good suck in the right place and he stopped in astonishment.

"What a smart boy!" Amy cheered and handed him a present of his own. "Would you like to start now," she gave her gift of the harmonica to David, "or wait 'till your son does it all for you?"

"Seems I've got no choice. All three of you, I bet all four of you, are set on having things your way!" Still he waited until we were almost through with opening our presents before he started on his.

It wasn't just what we gave to each other that I remember so well from that Christmas, it was the absence of tension. No one was worried, or testy. Amy didn't worry about her baby. I didn't feel closed in or annoyed with Sampson, or feel left out when they talked about their baby. David relaxed because we did, and spent the whole day with us, instead of escaping to his paints. Sampson gloried in the happiness and toys and pretty paper to throw around. David played checkers with me, and lost, but regained his "manly superiority" as he called it, when he beat Amy at chess. The chess set was his gift to her. She teased him into another game and they were still at it when

Sampson and I went to bed. Much, much later he woke me when he slid in beside me.

"Sorry," he whispered, "Didn't mean to wake you."

"It's ok," I whispered close to his ear, which, on impulse I nipped sharply.

"O Ho! Woman! Think you can get away with that do you?" He tweaked my nose, I grabbed his hand away. He made quick little bites at my throat; I was weak from keeping my giggling quiet and his hands to himself. Wanting him flushed through me so that I didn't, couldn't, didn't want to stop him. Sometimes I think of David, and that .. fulfillment .. that only .. sexual love can know....

That night too, is why I cherish that Christmas memory so. It was the only time we made love with Amy there in the house. Maybe if I'd been more unbending about that....

23. You Aren't Amy!

Aunt Sophie seemed confused. We were both embarrassed. I suggested we go to bed. The fire was about out and it was late.

"You're right," she said quietly, "it is late." We went to bed.

After breakfast next morning I eased her back into her memories as we worked on a couple of casual pants-suits I'd wear at work. My job is in a camera shop. I serve customers by day and have the use of the developing and printing equipment at night. It's an ideal setup because I can do my own printing of the shots I take on weekends and for special occasions of goings-on in town. The best ones I sell to our local newspaper. So far, the profits are small but I've reached the point where I receive more calls than I make, and that's encouraging.

I was anxious for Aunt Sophie to get her story finished. I wanted to know about Samson, why she'd left, why wasn't her son with her? It seemed more polite, and easier, to start with the second baby.

"Did Amy have her baby all right?" I asked as we spread the cloth on the dining table and began pinning the pattern in place.

"Oh, Amy's baby." She paused, distracted, and straightened up from the table, a pin held in mid-air. In her eyes was a question as she turned to me.

"Didn't I... No, I guess I didn't. Well," she bent again to the pattern and pushed the pin into the paper, joining it to the cloth. She picked up her story.

"The baby was due in early February. The doctor was going to come to the house when Amy started labor, that was the plan, but she came back from a visit to him in mid-January, upset.

It was raining, as usual, and she came in with water dripping from her hat and coat. She pulled her hat off and threw it onto the shelf above the coat rack. Sampson babbled to her from where he was holding onto the couch where he'd just pulled himself up. I helped her off out of the wet coat and hung it over a chair to dry. David sat her on another chair before the warming fire and undid her blond hair that fell to just below her shoulder blades. She moved her neck around as he lifted and separated the wet strands. He took the brush from where he kept it on the mantle above the fireplace and teased out the damp clumps at her forehead down to the ends of her hair. Taking the comb that always lay beside the brush he straightened her drying hair, separated it into three strands which he plaited into a single braid down her back. His hands were gentle and sure, they had done this task many times. Amy's breathing slowed as she relaxed with his touch. It always soothed her when he put his hands in her hair.

She turned to look at me. The doctor was leaving! She spoke in a rush, the words falling on top of each other.

"Sophie, he's going back to Portland! His father is old and not well and he says there's not enough of a practice for him here since the road work slowed down. There's not enough people here!" David stroked her shoulders to calm her.

I didn't see that there was much of a problem. After all, I delivered without a doctor and so did my mother.

"I'll bet," I said to her, "that your mother didn't have one either."

"No, but with my brother and sister, David's mother was there..."

I was hurt. "Amy! You know I'll be here! I've delivered all of Mandy's kids and they're all ok!"

"Oh, I know, Sophie." Her forehead wrinkled and she screwed up her mouth. She was trying to be calm but couldn't hide her worry. She was scared. "I do trust you! You know I love you, but I wish ... oh! I wish my mother was here!"

"She's not here! Mine wasn't either, you will remember! Looks like all you've got is me."

I was sorry for her distress at this unexpected turn but surprised that she was making such a fuss about it. I tried to soften my exasperation by adding, "And David. We've all been through this before. You'll see! It'll be all right!"

David hadn't said much till now. His hands stopped moving, resting lightly on her back. "You're not going to have the baby here." We both turned to look at him. "Doctor James said there's a good doctor in Seaside and that's where you're going."

"Seaside!" we said together. "That's over eight miles away!"

"It's closer than Portland and if a doctor can't come here then you will go to him." He struck the back of Sophie's chair with his fist, angry. She pulled away from his reach, her eyes looking at him, wide, startled.

He went on, "Some doctor! All the time promising to be here, and then, just when you need him, leaving you alone!"

I started to say again, "But she won't be alone. I wasn't alone. I'll be here, like you were with me!"

"You aren't Amy!" he said sharply, cutting me off.

I was hurt. I barely heard Amy's quick breath, "David!"

For a second he looked confused, then his voice fell as he reached out to me.

"I only meant..." His eyes were wet with the hurt that we both felt, and I'm sure now, with the fear he felt for Amy. "Sophie. You were, are, strong, and," he stumbled for words. "Oh, Sophie, If anything happened .. to Amy .. to the baby ...." His voice was low, serious.

You've got Sampson, I thought, unfairly, and guiltily, knowing I could never say it. I turned my head away. The thought had just popped in. I was as upset and tried to keep my hot face hidden. He put his hands on my shoulders and turned me toward him.

"I'm sorry. I wouldn't hurt you for the world, Sophie," his eyes were sad. "I love you. But this is different."

My first flash of jealousy at Amy's baby was gone, and I knew I was being foolish, though I didn't know why, yet.

"David," I said, straightening up. His hands fell from my shoulders but I reached up with my hand to his face, and touched his cheek lightly. "You're right." I looked at Amy. "I'm the one who is wrong. Of course I want what's best for Amy." The strained faces relaxed a little. "And for your baby." I added.

Briskly, I gathered my no-nonsense voice, (not unlike the one Amy used on me when she came to my cabin), stood up quickly. "And if it's a doctor in Seaside then I better get you ready."

Relieved, David said, almost cheerfully, "We all have to get ready. Four weeks for four people - five people..!" He stopped for a moment and pulled his shoulders back, as if adjusting a new weight. "In Resort City ... we have lots of work to do."

He could be so annoying. "David, you obviously haven't thought this out. How do you know it's going to be four weeks?"

"Two weeks 'till the baby comes and two weeks after for Amy and the baby to rest." He was smug about his mathematics. Amy and I looked at him. She spoke up first.

"It might be longer, it might be sooner. Babies don't always follow the schedules we set up."

I said, "You can't know for sure how long you'll be gone, and Sampson would drive us crazy cooped up in a strange place. It'll be easier on all of us and less expensive if he and I stay, though," I looked at Amy, "I wanted to be with you. But," I was confident, "You'll be ok, just fine."

And she was. They left a couple days later, grocer Puffin proudly driving them in his new Ford, glad of a reason to go somewhere and show off his new car ... and make a few dollars.

Amy gave birth to Lillian May a week after they got to Seaside, not much wiggle room in David's time-schedule. The baby, Lily, was perfect, but Amy was too weak for the trip back until nearly a month later. The labor turned out to be long and difficult. They'd been grateful for the medical assistance, and so was I. And in a silly, secret way, I felt superior - but the fact was that neither of us would have more children for David.

When he got home he pulled the Smither's family Bible from where they kept it in the top drawer of their bedroom chest and David added the birth of Lillian May to the chronicle. The births were done.

24. The Loneliest Weeks

The five weeks that they were gone were the loneliest weeks of my life. Worse even than the five months in the cabin, for then I'd had David at least once a day.

I popped corn, but it was tasteless. Sewing made me nervous. I worked on the "Beach" quilt and had it nearly finished. It was hard without someone to keep Sampson entertained while I sewed. I could only work on it when he was sleeping. I enjoyed it though as it had all fit together much better than I had imagined it would. And somehow working with the material I felt closer to that time when I had first been getting to know David, as if that barely-bearable tension I'd felt then was somehow stitched into the design, into the material even.

I found the house so quiet at night, too lonely to stay up much after Sampson had gone to bed. When I got to bed it felt so big for just me. Some nights I'd give in when Sampson wanted to get in my bed, not his. It was comfort to us both. After a few days he stopped looking around so much for them, but with the passing of time, I missed them even more, despite the fact that Sampson and I got really close during those weeks alone. He turned eleven months old while they were gone, every day of his growing brought a new experience for both of us! I established a new routine that met our needs better. We two were pretty casual about things, waiting until evening before washing up the day's dishes, things like that. Just sitting together while he nursed, for longer than I had when I'd had chores to attend to with Amy. I turned the chair to the window so we could look out at the ocean. It was peaceful as Sampson picked up my mood and nursed more quietly than his usual active way, watching with me as the ocean swelled and poured foam onto the shore.

But with no adults the days were often lonely and boring. About once a week I'd walk up to Puffin's store, carrying Sam, to get basic foodstuffs but more to have someone to talk to. The trips to the store always unnerved me some. We'd told Puffin the same story I'd told the boys that I was staying to housekeep and take care of David's wife during her pregnancy, and he didn't see either Amy or me when I was in the last of my pregnancy but still I felt uncomfortable living under the sharp eyes of Puffin and his wife, Mrs. P.

They were used to seeing the four of us together and accepted the story that Sampson was Amy and David's child. I was nervous about going there with the baby even though we had told the Puffins that it was easier for all if Sampson stayed with me while they were in Seaside for the delivery. To that end I even bought milk from them for Sampson but they didn't know that I used it to get him used to a cup but that his primary milk was from me.

The other reason to go to Puffin's store was to see if there were any messages or mail for me. There seldom was, but one day Amy's publisher sent finished copies of her first book, <u>Sampson, Boy of the Sea</u>, and I wrote her immediately. She answered, ecstatic with the birth of her healthy daughter, and a book in the same year.

The weather again got on my nerves, but for a different reason. Now there was no one to watch Sam when I went outside. He was walking around the furniture, flinging everything within reach to the floor. I thought he was going to drive me crazy. When he was awake I wanted him asleep and when he was sleeping the house was dead quiet and I wanted him awake. We fought over the bookcase. It fascinated him, I guess because, like a dog nuzzling old shoes when it's left alone, the books smelled of David and Amy. They 'played' with them, so did he.

That's how I started reading. One night when Samson had gone to bed early, tired after a day of chasing the cat around the house, wailing when I was outside and hanging on me when I was in, plus the usual mess he made . . . I was putting the books back in their place when I pulled out <u>Girl of the Limberlost</u> from under the dining table.

The cover was wet where he'd chewed on the edges so I left it on the table to dry. It was still there when I settled down to write Mom and Dad. I wrote them at least twice a month, telling them all about "Amy's baby". I'd already explained about the new one coming, making it sound like I'd come home if I could but that Amy was such a weakling that I couldn't just yet.

Everything seemed too quiet, inside and out. It made me twitchy. The book just laid there, it's chawed cover still dark from Sam's four slurpy teeth. Looking at it all I could think of was Amy and David sitting night after night reading by the fire. David often read out loud. I always wondered how they could sit like that, for hours sometimes. I was sure it'd drive me crazy.

But now, tonight, I was lonely for them, and like Samson, the next best thing was their books.

I put more wood on the fire, partially just to hear the crackle, settled down in David's chair with a thin quilt over my legs and a cup of hot tea on the little table beside his chair. I sat there for a while watching the flames, thinking over the last two years until I couldn't stand thinking anymore and opened the book.

You must remember that I'd never read anything but the Bible, and only parts of that, and a few schoolbooks, history and such that I found boring, so it took a while to get used to a story like that with no Chapter 1, Verse 3 or battles to remember but once I got over feeling wasteful about spending time on reading I got caught up in it. It took me a week or so to find out the girl was going to be all right, despite her crazy mother. And when I finished it I started another, about a strange boy, Little Shepherd of the Hills I think it was, and read that through, and then started on Moby Dick but it was hard reading and I never did finish it, though David tried to get me to.

25. PRE-T-T-Y!

They returned in first week in April: David, Amy, and beautiful little Lillian. As I said, about once a week Sampson and I walked into town, taking the steps David had cut into the hill behind the house up to the road. Cannon Beach wasn't much of a town, then, just a few buildings, plus the hotel.

The store had a phone where David was to call when Amy delivered or if he had any messages for me.

When I walked in, early that first week of April, both Sampson and I were cold from the mist. I sat down in the chair by the coal stove and unwrapped the baby. My arms were aching from carrying him. He was getting to be a big boy! It felt so good to sit down for a bit and just listen to Puffin's gossip. He didn't think it was gossip, of course. He told everyone who would listen that Mrs. P. told everything she knew and a lot that she didn't and that was why he never told her the messages that came through the phone. It wasn't true, she wasn't the gossip. It was a clear case of the pot calling the kettle black, but it did drive her mad that he never told her anything. She heard the news when we did, but, there was little she could do about it. He was tall and thin, spry, and she was short and heavy - she was downright fat, though I hate to say it.

I was there once when the phone rang and he nearly ran her over getting to it. Being agile like that he always beat her to the phone, no matter where he was! Mrs. Puffin moved slow, and breathed hard if she tried to speed up any. The name fit her. I always wondered what she was like when they got married, whether she had grown to fit the name or it was accidental. She was a good soul. When he told me about the baby she was as thrilled as I. The next time I came in she gave me a pink bonnet she'd made, trimmed with lace and embroidered with tiny roses, to give to Amy for Lillian.

Puffin would make his customers guess if there had been a call.

"Well, hello," he'd always say when you came in. If there had been a message his voice would have his important, I-have-a-secret tone that would attract your attention. You'd look at him curiously, which is what he wanted.

It irritated me that this self-important man would play with me so. If you got mad, "Ok, Puffin, out with it! Did somebody call?" he'd find something that needed doing in the back room. Make you wait.

"Mrs. P.," he'd call, "There's a customer out here for you." Since she knew less than you did about what message might have been left, the two of you would stumble around the subject, filling your order and awkwardly discussing the weather until he came back in, and, acting as if he'd suddenly remembered, "Oh, by the way! Would you believe it?"

No.

"I almost forgot! Hank Jenning's wife called couple a days ago, asked if you couldn't send your oldest boy, Tom isn't it?"

You would nod yes, exasperated, trying to speed him up.

"I remember the time he came in here wanting some perfume for that gal that wore the short skirts, and . . . huh! Anyhow Jenning's wife wants Tom to come out for a couple days to chop some winter wood for them. Seems Hank missed the log and got his foot instead. Ain't it a shame!"

You'd agree, yes it was, partially 'cause it was, and partially 'cause his voice didn't have that 'I've-finished-giving-the-message' tone and you were crazy to hear the rest!

"She said they have a young boar just right for slaughter and they'll give it to Tom in payment but you all will have to do the job 'cause Hank's in bed you know, feeling pretty bad I guess."

At this point you'd know by the deflated tone that you had all the message: you were going to have winter pork which Puffin knew you needed badly 'cause your sow had killed the spring litter before you'd found them.

Nevertheless I found it difficult this time to play his game.

"Mr. Puffin, have you heard from David?"

He narrowed his eyes at me and even Mrs. Puffin tilted her head.

"You know," he said slowly, "that's interesting, you calling Smithers by his first name right out like that. I always thought, 'course I never knew anybody before 'at had a housekeeper," his eyebrows and shoulders rose a bit to show his disapproval of this employment, "but I always thought they was Mr. and Mrs. to their help, huh?"

I didn't react to his suggestion that I might be more than a housekeeper, just sat quietly and looked at him calmly. I'm sure my eyes were flashing though because Mrs. Puffin started clearing her throat and he stopped playing the cat and mouse game with me.

"Well, how'd you guess I'd heard from Smithers? Guess you figgered they'd be back soon, huh?" I nodded.

"Well, well. You're right! Tomorrow in fact!"

I started, my mouth opening with surprise.

"Surprised ya, huh? Me too. I'd thought he'd want me to come pick them up but he got some fella there with a big ol-fashioned horse and buggy outfit who was coming over this way to visit his folks." He was obviously disappointed that he wouldn't get to show off his machine again.

"'Course I couldn't go now anyway. My busy time you know, people thinking about spring planting' and all, and getting ready for summer visitors." He always called them, 'visitors,' never tourists.

Tomorrow! I bought sugar, flour and chocolate. Puffin had just got a ham in from one of the farms and I bought that, too. I walked home in a mind fog. Samson seemed light, even with the groceries in the other arm. I laughed about nothing and he laughed with me. I started humming when we were on a flat space on the path and he started humming with me, singing with me! My heart just about burst right there, excited about wanting to share this latest trick of his with David. And Amy. Sampson's little mouth moved around trying to make the same sounds I was, it was so cute. Oh, he was adorable! I couldn't wait for Amy and David to be back to share him with. I was so full of excitement, the waiting of the last weeks was about to be over! We could get back to normal living. I'd clean the house.

Sampson saw flowers beside the path and he pointed down to them. "Pret-ty!" he said. I about dropped him in the excitement of his word! They were the first spring flowers we'd seen and the first word he said without prompting. We stopped right there and picked them. Sampson clutched them in his little fists all the way home which bent the stems but I knew David and Amy wouldn't care. I put them into a vase and told Sampson, "Don't touch. For Daddy and Amy." And he didn't, other than to just go up and touch the vase, and look at me and ask, "Pret-ty? Da Da?" I'd smile yes and he'd touch again with just the tip of his finger."

He was probably as happy to see me happy and not yelling at him as he was at the idea of Daddy and Amy. I don't think he knew what was happening. 'Tomorrow' didn't have much meaning to him, but he responded to my joy with his own smiles and when he went down for his afternoon nap he hummed himself to sleep.

I did love that boy.

26.   Daddy's Smile

When they pulled up late the next afternoon I had the ham baked, the cornbread keeping warm in the side oven. I was ready to heat some canned tomatoes from last summer's garden, and I baked a three-layer chocolate cake. Everything was waiting, as were Sam and I.

I grabbed my little boy and stuffed him into his coat. He wrapped his arms and legs around me and we ran down the steps to meet them.

That's the day everything changed.

I can't blame Lily, she was only a baby, but she stole my David away from me.

I'd thought David was silly and daddy-proud when Sampson was born but it was nothing compared to the way he made over that little girl!

When I saw him stepping from the buggy I thought my heart would bust. I hollered, 'Hello! Welcome back!' He turned to see me running towards him. He only had to take a couple of steps before he threw his arms around both of us. He smelled and felt so good! David couldn't kiss me with the driver right there but after a long hug he took Sampson and kissed him hard, laughing all the time.

"It's so good to be back! And look at my little Sampson! So big! Look Amy, how big he is!" And hugging him again he said to us both, "Boy did we miss you!"

Not, "I," but, "We." I didn't notice the difference until later.

"Sophie! David!" Amy called from within the coach, laughter in her voice, "Help us out!"

I went to the door and Amy handed me a bundle of warm baby. Lily was so wrapped up against the cold that I only saw a bit of her pink face through the opening in the blanket. David helped Amy out, one arm tight around Samson, who, frightened by all the noise, was squirming to get back to me.

Amy kissed me on the cheek and squeezed me, "Oh, Soph! I'm so glad to be here! We thought that ride would never end! I can't wait to get into the house. I'm so tired."

She looked wonderful to me, though her face was pale. Her hair was cut in a new style, curling softly around the edges of a new cap that fit close to her head. Her eyes sparkled as she smoothed the bundle I held. "We've got to get her inside so I can show you our treasure! And," looking at Sampson, "I've got some huggin' and squeezin' to do!"

Within a short time we had babies, adults, boxes and trunks moved down into the house. As soon as the door shut and we were all alone Amy took the baby and, laying her gently on the table, unwrapped the blankets, untied her knit cap, and lifted her gently to me.

"Lillian May, meet your Auntie Sophie."

I looked down into a face that was baby beautiful. Like Sampson, she had hair! Black curly hair that surrounded her tiny face. Lily's face was the color of rich cream, and she had bright rosy cheeks, but it was her eyes that were amazing.

"Look, Sophie," crowed David. "Amy's grandmother had violet eyes and I think Lily will too." He sounded like this was some special talent that he could take credit for!

"Here." He took the baby from me. "Watch this." He rocked her slowly up and down and tickled her under her chin. "Daddy's little dumpling going to smile for Aunt Sophie?" Her mouth twitched. She had David's mouth, and it spread out into David's big grin but with tiny dimples at the corners. Daddy's smile. He was too satisfied with himself. "Ain't she a corker?" But now the smile faded into a frown and she started crying. "Oh oh, Momma. I think our girl's hungry."

I settled Amy into her chair with her feet on the cushioned stool and David handed Lillian over. Amy unbuttoned the top of her dress and David watched with intense interest until the baby mouth found the nipple, stopped crying and started sucking.

"There," he said proudly, as if he'd done it himself, "Lily May sure knows where dinner is!"

After dinner for everyone was over (David didn't comment on the special cake, Amy did), we sat around the table and they, David mostly, told me all about Lillian's birth.

There'd been no special problem, just a very long labor, over 20 hours, which David threatened to repeat in length and detail until Amy interrupted him, "But it was worth it! I'd gladly go through it again, twice so, except ..." Her sentence was left unfinished. There was a short silence during which I looked from one to the other, wondering. David closed it.

"Right after she was born, as soon as it was 'decent' the nurse said, I went in and .. well, it's just a shame you weren't there. Amy was holding Lily and looking more beautiful than ever, if that's possible." He looked at her, she beamed at him; I felt like an intruder.

He continued on with detail after detail of Lillian's first weeks, her first feeding, her first bath, how she slept so quietly that it frightened him, on and on until Amy, exhausted, said, "David, I simply must go to bed."

We helped Amy and the baby upstairs. David put L.M., as he called her, in the cradle he'd made for Sampson and that I'd prepared before they came home. While he settled them I put Sampson to sleep in the small bed David had bought from a neighboring farmer, through Puffin.

Tired from the trip they both went to sleep quickly, though David hovered around Lily a while to make sure she was Ok till I laughed and said, "Come on, she'll be just fine. Let the poor babe sleep in peace. You're worse than a brand-new mother hen!"

He grinned that proud grin, "Yeah, I guess so, but ain't she fine?" he whispered as we went downstairs.

Frankly, I could hardly wait to get downstairs. I wanted to be alone with him. Wanted very much to be alone with him. You understand?

And he still hadn't kissed me. I was tired of waiting, so, before he could start unpacking or doing something else, I grabbed him and kissed him. He was surprised. I was seldom aggressive. But he didn't resist. He moaned but made me stop. That was a switch! I was confused and my feelings were hurt.

"I think we'd better take a walk," he said softly. I didn't say anything. He wasn't acting like my David. Was there something wrong with me? Or him?

I put on my heavy, hooded jacket and watched as he got the gas lantern from the hook by the door, put his 'souwester' on, then lit the lamp. His hands were unsteady, he had difficulty holding the match still.

I followed him out the door. We picked our way carefully down the path. When we got to the steep, tricky part at the end he handed me the lantern, felt his way carefully, took the lamp to set on the sand, and held out his arms. I nearly knocked him over wrapping my arms around him. He wasn't a big man but he stood strong, caught me and held me so tight I had to loosen his grip to breathe.

We left the lantern wedged between rocks near the path and walked. He put my right hand in his left and put them both deep in his coat pocket. We walked like that endlessly, along the water line with only a light moon to show the way. The roar of the surf and a harsh wind swept away the questions I cried aloud.

"What's the matter, David? Don't you care anymore?" I didn't dare say, 'love'. What if he said, 'No'? Besides, his kisses were more loving than ever, so that couldn't be it. It couldn't!

It didn't matter. My questions went unanswered as if he didn't hear but finally he turned and ran his fingers down across my lips, gently, to silence me. We walked for a long ways before he veered off the low tide to a sheltered place along the bank, where we sat down on the damp sand and held each other without speaking, until I began to get angry. He was acting so strange, and yet not at all like a man who had quit loving.

"Ok, David, what is it! What the hell's the matter with you?" It was dark and I always could swear easier in the dark, I don't know why.

"Nothings the matter! You don't have to be mean about it!" Now he was offended. I ignored his complaint.

"I just would like an explanation, that's all. One minute you're hot, the next cold . . what's going on?"

"Well, Sophie. To be truthful," - I wanted all of that - "I don't mean to have more children."

"What?" I wasn't sure I'd heard right.

"Sophie," he pleaded. "Listen, please. For twelve years I had one wife and no children and now all at once I have two wiv.. well, I have both you and Amy, and now Sampson and Lillian, and," he threw his hands up from my shoulder, "it's enough," he said so quietly I had to lean closer to hear his words.

That was all! He didn't want any more kids, so we couldn't . . but surely there was a way . . ! Besides, "Sampson is almost a year old and we've . . I'm not pregnant, so . . . "

"Don't be stupid!" he said sharply. "Can't you see how foolish we've been. There's only one sure way . . when people don't want any more children . . well, they don't! That's all. They stop!"

I knew better than that. "David." I couldn't believe he was so ignorant, "There are ways." I didn't know what they were but I expected he could find out. It wasn't my place. After all, he was older, certainly more experienced! And, I was a woman. An unmarried woman. Where was I to go to find out?

"Sure, there are ways, but I'm not taking any chances right now. The doctor told me Amy shouldn't have any more children. When I asked, 'How,' he just said to leave her alone for a few months then come see him late this summer and he'd tell me what we could do.

And," he added, "If Amy and I can't . . I don't think you and I . . should . . it wouldn't be right."

"But, what about me?" He hadn't demanded an answer right then. Never considered me.

"I couldn't. It didn't seem right. After all, Amy had just had the baby . . it was so long . . she was, is, in no condition for love-making . . he said another baby might kill her!"

The responsibility of being a minister's son always fell on him at the wrong time.

"Well, I'm sure glad you didn't seem over-anxious!" I said sarcastically, standing up and brushing the damp sand from my clothes. He jumped up.

"But, I still love you as much as ever! Nothing's changed." I looked at him. "Well, a little. But, I'll fix it, you'll see!" He tried to laugh. "After all, bigger men than I . . ." He stopped when I started laughing.

He went to bed with Amy that night and the next night he was back with me but I found his closeness almost worse than when he wasn't there. Now I was willing, even with Amy in the next room. But he wasn't! It just didn't seem fair!

27. A Long Narrow Box

The room was dark and chilly with only coals from the fire sending a red glow into the room. I looked at Aunt Sophie who was getting up slowly.

"We're going to have to turn the heat on tonight. Got those berries done just in time."

She went to the window and pulled the curtain aside.

"It's starting to rain." She ran her hand slowly back over her head, then brushed down the front of her dress and apron, as if wiping away old memories. "Been dry too long anyway, I like to see it rain."

She turned on a light over a small table in the corner. The table with the drawer that no children could get into. She always told us, "I keep my private things in there and if you don't get into my things I won't get into yours."

Aunt Sophie could be real nasty if we got into her 'pocketbook', or opened her mail, so we learned not to. And we could trust her not to pry into our lives either, consequently we told her many things we couldn't tell our parents, and left things at her house we didn't want them to see.

She pulled the drawer open slowly, her hands trembling with fatigue and emotion. She took out a long, narrow box and set it on the table. She felt under the drawer until she found something - a key was taped to the underside. She pulled it loose and slowly, her hands more steady, unlocked the box, lifted the lid and started to reach into it but put the lid down and walked slowly across the room, to me. She put the box in my hands.

"Here, you look through it if you want to. I'm going to bed."
There were lines in her face that I'd not seen before. She looked old, and sad. I was seeing her for the first time as the adult she now trusted that I was.

"I'm too old, and tired. It was all a long time ago. I don't know if I even care anymore." I wanted to say, you brought it up, I didn't, but I just held the box, feeling the comfortable weight in my hands. She went into her bedroom off the living room.

I left the box on my chair, added some wood to the fire and went into the kitchen to make some instant cocoa. When I got back her door was closed. No light showed underneath so I settled with the box into the familiar old chair.

28. Brittle, Yellowed Letters

The pungent fragrance of cedarwood was strong when I opened the box. In a neat stack lay a collection of old newspaper clippings and letters, the painful record of love awry. Only a few items appeared to have been handled much. I'd guess the others were simply put away and not touched again, being the kinds of things it is difficult to keep, but impossible to throw in the trash.

I read the papers as I came to them, in the order they'd been placed in the box.

On top was the obituary (Seaside paper) of David Smithers, local artist, born 1884, died August 1964. This was much handled and tear-stained. It listed as survivors: Son, Jonathan S. Smithers, of Cannon Beach, and daughter, Lillian M. Lawnrose, teacher in Laramie, Wyoming. Grandchildren David Smithers of Damascus, Ore., Wanda and Edward Lawnrose of Depoe Bay, Ore., and great-grandchildren Amy and Alica Smithers, Damascus, and Greg and Jenny Lawnrose, Depoe Bay.

I put David's obituary aside and picked up the paper underneath: Amy's death notice, July 1964. Listing the same survivors as David. Had David died because without her there was no longer a reason to live? Surely not. Perhaps. I wondered. No cause of death was listed for either.

I wondered too about the house. Was it still there or had it been torn down to make way for an A-frame, or more likely, turned into a Gift Shoppe of Unusual and Rare Items From the Sea, with parking space behind the building? Asphalt over Sophie's cabin. I looked at the next item, an envelope.

It was a letter from her son, written at sea, the date placing it during World War 11. It appeared to have been opened only once and then put back. The pages were fresh, the pencil writing clear and unsmudged.

I read:

On one of Uncle Sam's ships headed for only the Brass knows where.

Dear Mother,

It seems strange to call someone besides Mother Amy as Mother, but you are my mother, so I will.

This whole letter might seem strange to you, after so many years of not hearing from me but I've seen some bad things in this war and it seems to me if I can only make one thing right in this world at least that's one less wrong, and maybe every little bit helps. I hope so.

I'm writing about that letter I wrote to you on my 14th birthday. I'm sorry. I didn't mean it. I guess I meant it at the time but I'm older now and I hope not so stupid. Dad and Mom don't know what I said, they thought it was the usual thank-you note.

When I come back, if I come back, I've seen some awful things and sometimes a person gets scared, but, when I come back I want to come see you. Would that be all right with you? I would just like to see you and talk with you for awhile.

Well, I've got to go now. Wherever we are going it must important. The Brass is closed mouthed but we have our ideas. I will probably be all right. I've been lucky so far.

Please write soon if you would like to see me. Even if that's not possible I would like to hear from you.

Love,

Jon S.

There were no later letters from him. No clue as to whether she'd replied, or not.

I set the mail aside and drank my cold cocoa staring into the flames of Sophie's stove. I sat there for a while before opening the next letter that I could see was from John, one he'd written at fourteen:

April 4, 1933

To Miss Elm,

As you can see it's my birthday. I'm 14 years old now. Do you care? Don't think that just because you send me a card and some money once a year that I care anything about you! If you really cared about me you would come see me. You could at least send a present but I guess it's too much trouble for you to find out what a 14 year old boy likes and it's certainly too much trouble to write and ask me. But I guess you are too busy. I wouldn't write back anyway.

Probably you just don't care, so I don't either!

Do not send me any more money! Just forget about me like I have forgotten about you. I have my own Mother, and Father to give me money. They love me to. But you don't know about that because you are just a phony mother.

Don't send me any more cards either.

Your ex-son

Jon S. Smithers

Children have a good sense of where to hit to hurt - near the same place where they feel their own pain.

It was a relief to see that the next envelope was a Christmas card signed, "All our love, David, Amy, Sampson and Lily."

Written on the back was simply:

Hoping you are well. We are all fine here, we are very busy. Found these photographs, thought you might like to have them.

Love, Amy

p.s. I took the one of David and the children last summer on the beach, the other we had taken when David sold a painting a few years back of some tourists (should I say 'summer visitor's?'? ha ha) poking around the tide pools at Haystack.

Between my books and David's paintings we sell enuf to keep body and soul together and once in a while do something special, thus the studio photograph.

The pictures and the last two envelopes all looked as if they'd been handled often, yellowed and finger marked. I searched the photos closely. The studio photo revealed little of the personalities of the people, only that they were all very attractive. Amy looked more stern than Aunt Sophie had described her, but then so do most photos from that time. She looked contented, secure. Her eyes were clear and looked directly into the camera. David appeared to be a normally attractive man with interesting bushy eyebrows that Aunt Sophie had never talked about. Maybe they had gotten bushy with age. His eyes had a twinkle that came through the black-and-white photo and caught my attention.

As they had for Sophie.

The children were young, probably eight and nine or so; they were childishly attractive. Sampson resembled his father but had the black, black hair of Aunt Sophie's youth.

The other was more revealing of their personalities. The three of them wore bathing suits, mid-30's style I'd guess. David stood in the middle holding a beach ball high in the air and the children on either side reaching to grab it. Though obviously posed as all three were looking into the camera, their casual attitudes revealed more than a studio seriousness. All were grinning broadly and I stared at David. His hair was wild about his head, his face tanned and the grin was heart-stopping - and he was at least 50 by then. Jon and Lily looked like him, full of fun, but fresh, eager. Lily had long dark braids, dusty eyes, and a perfect figure. John was no taller than his dad but more muscular, and again, the black curly hair that marked him as Aunt Sophie's. Most remarkable was the full, good-natured intelligence shared by the trio and caught by the camera.

I finally put the pictures back in the card and added them to the pile.

There were only two envelopes left. The first was another letter from Jonathan-Sampson when he was only seven.

April 4, 1926

Dear Mommy Sofie,

How aur you? I am fin. Mommy show me yur pixure toda Daddy drew me an you wen i was a babi. Mommy say i growed in yur timi. Thats funni! Mommy say you luv me. i luv you to. i in skool now. Secon grad. Mommy say i spel awfl. Daddy say i to smart! Well, got to go now. Mabe i see you ths sumr. i 7 yers old toda.

Thank your four car and too dolar.

Luv

JONATHAN SAMPSON SMITHERS

Last, and explaining much, was a letter from David.

October 12, 1921

My dearest Sophie,

It's been over a year now since you left and I still miss you terribly, especially when the sea is stormy and I walk lonely on the beach. Amy comes sometimes but with the children it is hard for us both to get out together. Getting them both to sleep at the same time is hard. They both sleep in your old room and when it's daytime they just keep jabbering at each other and won't take their naps until we put one of them in our bed. And when they do sleep and we go out, Amy is nervous the whole time that they will wake up and fall down the stairs or something so we don't get many walks alone.

Love, are you ever coming back? I didn't believe you when you said you wouldn't return but it's been so long. You can't know how much I miss you or you wouldn't stay away. Surely you would be happier with us than with your sister. If you want children to take care of we certainly have them here! Sampson kept looking for you after you left. And so did I. My heart aches with wanting you.

Are you still making your beautiful quilts? The Haystack one is on our bed now and Amy often says how lovely it is and how nice it makes the room look and wants you to know we are taking good care of it.

It's cloudy and stormy today. One of the kind you didn't like too much but that I like best.

Sampson is well. He had a couple of colds last winter but that's all. He is talking up a storm and we have to watch him all the time he is awake or he is out the door and down the hill to the water. But don't worry, we put a lock high up on the door so he can't do that anymore!

We take L.M. with us to Puffing's and I think she's helping our credit there. Puffing is as proud of her as if he had done more than just drive her mother to Seaside!

Amy says to say hello and tell you to come visit anytime. She means come back soon, like I do. She is working now on a story about a little girl named L.M. (guess who) who travels about the world with her parents and has a special affinity for communication with dogs and cats which of course leads her into all sorts of adventures. Amy hopes to work it into a series like the Sampson books.

Please write us and tell us how you are. If you can't come now at least let us know how you are doing.

<u>Miss you awfully</u>!

All my love,
David

I read the letter twice. I didn't know whether she had answered but since none of the other letters had any reference to seeing her,

156

and there were no other letters from David I guessed he'd failed to win her back with emotional calls.

How strong she was! Or was it just stubbornness? I knew from the way she looked and sounded when she talked of him that her love had not died. Nor had her love for her baby left her. So what had she done with it?

That answer I knew. It had gone to Boyd most directly and to the others of us who were rocked in her arms and warmed in her bed and listened to when we had long complicated dreams and stories to tell. And later on, our loves were brought before her, the pain and joy shared in return for a soft shoulder or a sharp comment that we resented at the time but that would come back in the dead of night and focus our own questions on his, or her, or our, actions. Once we married though, her advice and soft shoulder disappeared. In fact, if she voiced an opinion at all it was in favor of the other person!

"I think you could perhaps try patience - you've never been very patient. Now that you're an adult it's way past time you stopped thinking of yourself so much!"

With advice like that you soon stopped asking. After all it was obvious she didn't know what she was talking about. She'd never been married! As far as we knew she had never even been in love! We teased her to find out but she would only say, "There's some things for me to know and you to wonder about."

I wasn't married yet, but I planned to be soon and I knew Aunt Sophie didn't approve of Len. She worried about his temper. We argued constantly about every little thing and he didn't like my new job either. Since we were going to be married soon anyway why did I need a career? She warned that a possessive man before marriage can become even more jealous after the vows are taken, and . . . .

I'd stopped talking to her about him. She'd never been in love! She didn't know how his eyes, his hands, and his concern about me made me feel! Now in the dark and cold room I wondered at her reason for exposing her—self, the deep self she'd kept hidden all these years. Why to me, now? Sure, I'd always listened better than the other cousins to her stories and had spent more time with her, but there was more to it than that.

I decided to think about it tomorrow after I'd left. Right now I was going to turn the heat on and go to bed. But first I put everything back in the box, locked and returned it to its' place in the drawer and left the key on the table. There was the boy to have the answer about tomorrow, too. Cannon Beach? Could it be that he still lived there? He would be old - impossibly old. An old boy? As much as the answers intrigued me, I dreaded asking her the question. I didn't want Sampson to be old, but neither did I want him to be dead.

29. No Escape

The next morning dawned bright and clear. Sun through the kitchen window reflected off the chrome edging of the table. The key was gone.

Perhaps we could forget the whole thing. She had left them all and I was sure the reason could be applied to my situation in some oblique way. Why else was she telling me this story? Almost everyone was dead and gone, it was morbid to rehash old wounds, what happened fifty years ago couldn't have any current relevance to me. Now, with my senses alert to a reason behind the telling, I was eager to be gone. I was not going to listen to unwanted advice, however indirect.

I'd just grab a cup of coffee and be gone.

But she was quicker than I. "Well, good morning, sleepyhead." It wasn't even 7:00 o'clock yet! Before I could finish, "Just a cup of coffee please, I've got to run," she was at the stove.

"Get some bacon and eggs into you and then I have a favor to ask before you go."

"Well, Aunt So," I hedged, "I just wanted to get some coffee…" but she cut through it.

"Nonsense! You need more than coffee. I'll make you a good breakfast!" I kept quiet. She was herself again, full of energy and hustle, not the old woman I'd seen the night before.

"Now, if after breakfast you could stay for awhile and help me with these windows, I'd sure appreciate it."

"The windows? But you always told me not to wash them when the sun is shining on them 'cause they streak."

159

"That was when I didn't need any help and could wait until a cloudy day. But," she bent her head to look feeble, "Now when a strong body that can reach up and isn't afraid of breaking old bones from falling off a chair comes around I just have to grab it and make use of it!"

I was wearing short sleeves and she laughed and squeezed the muscles in my right arm. Her fingers were softly rough, a contradiction but there she was, defined by the feel of her skin. She was pulling out all the stops again so I gave in. After all, maybe she was telling the truth.

"You know," she said as she put the coffee in front of me, "I always did like clean windows!" I'd never particularly noticed it. "In fact I was washing windows the day I decided to leave."

There it was! She was going to continue with the story despite the fact that I'd not brought it up.

30. Nightmare

When they brought Lily home I was so happy to have them back! I laughed and teased David about his obsession with the child. But the problem wasn't him, it was in me, and the situation. I was possessive and jealous, not unlike your Len. (Aha! This reference to him confirmed my suspicions - she questioned his character.)

Before Lily came, Sampson was the center of our attention. We all loved him but because I'd given him to David, I felt that we had a special closeness. I never saw resentment in Amy of that closeness. She accepted it, with an occasional envy that I saw now and then, but she wasn't mean-spirited. She seemed as happy for David as he was. But "their" baby brought a change to our lives. He paid more attention to Lily and Amy than he did to Sampson and me. I was still nursing Sampson but David didn't crowd around and crow over us anymore. Now it was Lily and Amy who got this attention.

Then she got the colic. Sampson had never been sick a day in his short life so when Lily cried in pain David couldn't stand it! For weeks he walked the floor with her at night. He wouldn't let Amy or I do it. "You have enough to do in the day taking care of these babies," he said to us, "I'll take care of Lily at night. You both need your rest. You can't get worn down." Her crying and the long nights were exhausting on all of us. Even through my sleep I could hear her when she woke up and started crying.

During the day we were all tired but it was only my temper that got short. They'd waited so long for a baby no sacrifice was too tiring for them. Amy kept saying, "This will pass. We just have to wait it out. Think of poor Lily. It's harder on her than us."

I wasn't sure. They were spoiling her terribly, but I said nothing.

Somewhere in her fourth month the colic eased but it was already too late for me. Probably if it hadn't been that straw it would have been something else. I couldn't share someone so close to my heart. Amy and David could, but I couldn't. They had each other and Lily in a way that would never include me. I wanted David and Sampson to be all mine. To care mostly about me.

That was never going to happen. David was a good talker, he'd convinced me this could work for all of us, but the reality was that it worked well for him, and Amy too in some ways - would she have Lily if not for me and Sampson? I was extra. I wasn't needed. David had manipulated me. I knew I had to take some responsibility too, I'd gone along with David's scheme in truth because it was the only way I could get what I wanted: David. I kept my thoughts to myself but inside I seethed with anger and tears.

I couldn't take my frustration out on Lily - she was so tiny! - or David or Amy (I was too afraid of losing him), so I took it out on the one person I had that was mine, Sampson.

I decided he was going to be potty trained and weaned off me. And stop pulling things from tables and bookshelves. And mind my every word! He was going to be a perfect little man. He wasn't ready for the sudden change and my anger toward him made it worse. You would think my experience with Mandy's kids would have taught me that children move slowly or quickly according to their own pace. Forcing your schedule on them it seldom works. But they'd been Mandy's children, not mine. I'd had to accept doing things her way which, since we had the same upbringing, was not all that different than mine. But I saw things that I would do different if they were mine, I wouldn't have put up with half the nonsense she did. The difference was that she had four little ones close together, I had only one. He was all mine, and now my full attention went to him.

When he wet his pants I spanked him and shamed him. "You big baby! Naughty dirty boy!" David and Amy were angry, with me.

"He's only a baby!" Amy said, almost crying.

David just looked at me and took Sampson away from me, holding him on his lap and rocking him. "It's all right. You'll do better next time."

Sampson not only didn't do, 'better next time,' he got worse. He started wetting the bed again, which he'd stopped when he was about a year old. So I had to put him back in night diapers, which he fought because I shamed him so about it. "No, no," he'd cry, trying to wiggle away. It got to the point where only Amy could do it because he ran away from me.

Weaning him was awful, too. If I'd just eased into it with him he might have given in but one morning as he started to climb into my lap I just said, "No, you're a big boy now. Eggs and cereal and a cup for you!" He fought it. He threw up. He knocked the cup to the floor and reached for me but it didn't work because soon there was nothing there. At first my breasts swelled and hurt and I'd say .. I remember it and am ashamed, "This hurts me more than you. You hurt Mommy!"

David got very angry when I said that. "You have no right! Can't you see what you're doing to him? What is the matter with you?"

"Don't interfere. He's mine. You take care of Lily, I'll take care of Sampson."

I didn't look at his face when he said, "He doesn't 'belong' to anyone. He is his own."

Thus I brought screaming and crying to what had been a peaceful house. 'The matter' with me was that I was blind jealous. This sharing didn't work for me, maybe it would of if I'd been brought up to it, but I wasn't. It didn't work for me in our little Cannon Beach family.

As long as I, through Sampson, was the primary recipient of David's attention I was happy. Only I had been able to provide him with a child. But now I had to share this glory, and be happy about it! It wasn't in me.

When it comes to our own child most of us are blind. The child must be perfect! We all go about trying to make perfect children in our different ways. One believes in the belt, another in a kiss, another counsels a mixture between the two. Perhaps one method will work, but when you have three people, three ways in conflict, the mixture doesn't work.

It certainly didn't work with Sampson. He became impossible. Now we had two crying babies, and three exhausted, tense, and angry adults.

Maybe if I'd still had David's physical love I'd have been different, but it was gone, even the hugs and kisses disappeared. I grew more frantic, my determination and anger got more with Sampson, and the gentle love play with David dried up. There were many nights when he didn't come to my bed at all, the excuse being at first that he had to be up with Lily, and when he was there .. the intimacy wasn't. Always I thought, tomorrow night .. But it didn't happen.

And there was something else, something I didn't see until later. Always I'd made quilts, as my sisters did, but with me it had been more ... an obsession almost. Where my sisters sewed out of duty and need, to me it was a joy. With David and Amy's appreciation my 'stitching' took on a new meaning for me. I was an artist! Creative! But there was no time or energy for quilting. The scrap bag by my bed was in the way. I stumbled over it and Sam got into it. I shoved it under the bed. Once in a while I'd sweep under the bed, and hit the bag making the dust fly.

Nothing but babies. I loved babies, but ....

In my confusion I looked for someone to blame. It must be because of Lillian. I didn't blame her, I told myself in my lonely bed (just as lonely when David was in it now as when he wasn't), but before she came ... if she hadn't come ... if she hadn't been born ... if she went away ... but my thoughts stopped there, guiltily.

And then I got a letter from my sister Lydia. She wrote that her twin, Lucy, was getting married in September. Lucy and Jack were planning a honeymoon at the beach in Seaside. Did I know a nice place they could stay in Cannon Beach for a couple of days? I wasn't sure whether this was a thin excuse to get me to invite them to stay over with us - I could easily sidestep that. It wasn't my house. They thought I was the housemaid who took care of the kid. I read and re-read the letter until the sweat on my hands smudged Lydia's neat writing. I put the letter away in my bedroom drawer where I wouldn't be running into it.

I didn't like the idea of Lucy being there at all. I didn't know this Jack (who turned out to be one of Zed's barflies), but Lucy was sharp-eyed and sharp-tongued. It would be impossible to explain why Sampson called me Mommy, and he looked too much like me for comfort.

One morning in early August I was washing windows and thinking about the problem. Sampson had become impossible. I was washing the living room window that opened to the sea and watching a couple walking arm in arm on the beach. It was windy and they were snuggled close together. My heart hurt to see them. The pail of water was by my feet and Sampson just walked over and deliberately, I'm sure of it, pushed it over onto my feet. I jumped and would have slapped him if the shock of the warm water hadn't suddenly triggered a memory. The water and the couple on the beach revived a fragment of the nightmare I'd had the night before and forgotten by morning.

In the dream I was walking out into the ocean, carrying a baby, Sampson. He was wrapped in a partially finished quilt. The waves didn't get us wet. I wasn't cold. It was very peaceful. Without warning a huge wave swept over us and when it was gone so was the baby, but not the quilt. I looked frantically for the baby but I couldn't find him so I ran back to the house screaming, "David! David! Sampson's gone!"

He looked at me oddly and said, "No he's not. He's right here." And there he was, smiling and cheerful playing on the rug.

"Well, then, where's Lillian?"

"Lillian?" he asked, "Who's Lillian?"

"I guess it was Lillian I lost," I said, "but that's all right because now we'll all be happy again."

Amy came up and kissed me on the cheek. "You're probably right but it was an awful thing you did."

I smiled and let the quilt float down to cover up Sampson.

That was all I remembered but it was enough make me know ... I was wishing the baby dead. And Sampson gone? Right then I made my decision to go. It would also solve the problem of what to do about Lucy and Jack.

I could see from the expressions of relief on David and Amy's faces what they had feared I'd do to Sampson for dumping the pail over, when instead I just got the mop and cleaned up.

The sooner I left, the better. I decided just that quick. When I'd come to the point of wishing a child dead, perhaps both of them, I knew it was all wrong. They were still watching me as I put the mop away. We were all quiet, even Sampson. I think Amy sensed it. My face always betrayed me.

"I have to leave." I didn't know how else to say it. There was no sense edging around it. David was the first to react. Maybe Amy was waiting to take her cue from him, to see what he wanted.

"What are you talking about? Leave? Leave where?" But he knew what I meant. And there was no conviction in his voice. I think he was relieved.

"Here and now." Maybe I'd hoped for pleading, tears ... if he'd begged me to stay, maybe ... but he didn't.

Surprisingly, to me, for I would not have done the same in her place, Amy came over and put her arms around me. "Sophie, it's not necessary. Give it a few days thought. You'll see I'm right." For the second time I saw the look of sadness I'd seen only once before, the night she took me into her home.

"No. I've got to do this. I can't go on."

"It's been all right," David protested. He had to defend his position. I raised my eyebrows. "It has been a little rough lately." He could have said,' You've been rough,' but he didn't. But I knew and so did they.

"Maybe it's been all right for you and Amy, but not for me."

He started to protest but I stopped him. I shook my head and put my hand against his mouth.

"I just can't do it. I tried." I looked from him to Amy. "We tried. And it didn't work." I moved towards her but the look in her eyes stopped me between them.

Her eyes were guarded, her jaw firm and fierce. Fear. She swallowed, and stepped towards me. It was odd but what I noticed was the sound of the wind moving through the trees outside the window. Moving through us as well.

"What about Sampson?"

I knew the answer to that. I'd always known it, from the first time I saw her holding him. She loved him as much as I did, perhaps more, different. The only way I could keep my vow to protect him was to give him up. She would be a better mother to him.

"Sampson will be just fine. Here. With you."

"Sophie," she moved towards me now, her eyes and face softening, "Be sure. Are you sure you want this? Are you sure you know what you're doing?"

"I know. It doesn't matter that I wish it were different. I joined into this 'arrangement' against my better judgment. You can give him what I can't - two parents. At home he'd be considered a, you know."

David winced.

"And people here think he's yours and my people think so too. It would only make things terrible for him if I took him with me. Please understand."

Amy didn't understand. She struggled to keep a neutral face but the tightness around her eyes and face relaxed. She would never understand but she agreed to my decision. Sampson was hers too. I don't think Amy would have ever left her child, which was why I felt safe leaving him with her. That doesn't mean I think I was wrong. Circumstances are different for everyone and in our case it would have hurt him more to take him with me into a world that would never have seen him as I did. Today things are different, and maybe I'd do different, but I don't know. Water under the bridge.

31.   You'll Be Back.

Amy helped me pack. I didn't take much besides my clothes, some shells, Sampson's booties that I'd made before he was born, and my scrap bag.

David went into town and arranged a ride for me with a couple that was going over to Seaside, where I could catch the train to Portland. When he came back I was ready. Amy came downstairs with the "Ocean" quilt.

"Sophie. You forgot this."

"No. It's Sampson's. Keep it. Maybe he'll want it someday. Tell him you got it from a lady who helped take care of him when he was a baby."

"I'll do no such thing! How, pray tell, would we explain you to Sampson when you come back?"

"I won't be back."

"Sure you will," David spoke up, turning from the door where he was setting my trunk and boxes before carrying them up to the road where the Seaside people were picking me up. "As soon as you get to Portland you'll realize your mistake and when you do, I want you to come right back." He'd decided to act as if the whole thing was just a temporary situation and that when I came back I'd be fine again and so would everything else. Whether he really believed that or not ... for a bright man he was good at deceiving himself. And me for a while.

A horn honked from up the hill. Mercifully the children were asleep. I went upstairs while David and Amy carried my baggage up the hill.

Lillian was lying beside Sampson, her feet jammed into his back. I straightened her out, moving my hands against her legs ever so softly; she stirred slightly. I kissed her forehead, "I'm sorry little one."

Sampson was hard to leave. I tucked the light blanket up around his shoulders and felt the little muscles in his arms. I leaned over quickly and kissed the back of his neck; I can taste it today, warm and salty. "Goodbye little love, Son. Be happy."

Blindly I got out of the house and wiped the tears away before I got to the car. But they started again. I hugged Amy hard. She had tears, too. "Good luck, dear Sophie."

And then, despite the couple who were watching all this with big eyes I threw myself in David's arms and kissed him wildly. "David! I loved you so much!"

"Please come back, Sophie. Please." He held me tight. "I love you too."

I got in the back seat as quickly as I could, a curtain of tears between me and them.

"Please, let's go now." I was sobbing. It was terribly embarrassing. I was crying in front of strangers!

We left.

It took forever to get to Seaside. The couple gave up trying to have a conversation with me. They were kind, she patted my shoulder, he helped me with my ticket and with getting onto the train. I barely know how it was done.

I sat alone looking at the different greens and shapes of trees as we passed through the forests. The train was slow, nevertheless I was in the Portland station before I was ready. Would I have ever been ready? Before getting on the streetcar I called Amanda in Gresham to have Zed meet me when I got off the trolley. They were glad to have me back because Amanda was about due with Boyd and we had our hands full, what with all the kids, and the canning and the new baby, and such....

I've been here most ever since but a part of my heart has always been in the fog and mist of the coast, with my other family.

32. Some Things To Remember

Aunt Sophie said, "And now," with no particular emotion in her voice, as if she hadn't just been telling me that extraordinary story, "you better be on your way or you'll be late." She walked me to my car.

"Wait," I said after I hugged her, "did you ever regret it? Didn't you ever go back, see them, see Sampson, or David, or Amy?"

"Of course I regretted it!" She looked away, but simply, as if examining a dying rose bush. "Almost as soon as I got to Mandy's, as David said I would. I missed Sampson terribly. I worried constantly, for a long time. Whenever a letter came I feared something might have happened, and when I didn't hear, it worried me even more. I suffered terribly. You can't imagine. There was no one to talk to. I had to hold it all in, pretend everything was perfectly normal. But at night when everyone was asleep I tormented myself, asking myself whether what I did was right or wrong. Whether I'd wronged Sampson. The guilt was the hardest to live with."

Her eyes again turned to me. She looked at me clearly, directly. "And no, I never went back. I had enough to do here, and after I waited a few months .. it would have interrupted too many lives."

"But the cards, the letters?"

"Oh, at first I wrote often and they wrote back, and then, oh we wrote at Christmas time, like people do, and," she nodded, "you saw the letters. Too much hurt."

She opened the car door for me to get in. "There is a little more to tell, and I think you want to know."

"About Sampson?"

"Yes, but now you've got to be on your way!" She was now very anxious to close it and have me gone. I put my hand on the door to hold it open.

"Tonight, I have free time after I get off work. I won't be able to sleep unless you tell me. He's my cousin! Ok, tonight, after work? I'll pick something up from the grocery and feed you dinner, ok?"

"All right. But don't worry about dinner. I'll make that stew that you like."

At that I let her close the door. I rolled down the window. "I'll pick up some bread. You've got to let me do something." It was always so hard to do something for Aunt Sophie.

"All right, you bring the bread. We'll have stew and bread."

"And Sampson. We'll have Sampson for dinner, too?" At that she smiled such as I'd never seen from her, not even when she'd first began talking about David. Clear deep in her eyes.

"Yes, Sampson," she agreed. "Then you'll know it all." She rolled her eyes. "Get going now!" she said and whacked the hood of my car with the flat of her broad hand. She made me laugh.

Thinking about her mystery as I made my way through the heavy noon-hour traffic I was amazed at the number of clues her house held to that past life. The quilt on the upstairs bed with embroidered shells and the outline of Haystack Rock, the two small children at the base looking at the tide pools. The shells in the kitchen. And the booties on the dresser in her bedroom. We'd teased her about a past love, but never seriously. It had been a joke. I wondered now how she had felt when we teased her. "Poor old Aunt Sophie" had always been there for us.

Sure, she supported herself with her sewing machine, doing mending and alterations, and quilting, quilting, quilting until we wondered that her eyes didn't give out, but no one in the family ever gave it serious consideration. We were proud when she won a first prize at the State Fair one year for one she made out of ties, but we never took it as serious as she did. Even when the demand for her creations took off so that she was able to sell the large backlog that she had and had more work than she had hours for, we counted it as just luck. Never thought of it as 'art'.

What could be more important than our lives, what we thought about this and that? It was her purpose to be there for us. We never questioned it. I'd been as selfish as Len was, what made us happy should make her happy too.

After work I headed to her house for dinner and story. My thoughts returned to her when I stopped at the deli for a loaf of bread. How about rye? Not what we usually had with her stew, and not something I would have bought for her before though I was fond of it, but now I thought of her in a different way. A woman with experience in the varieties of life, indeed more experience than I, a 20th century woman.

When I pulled into her driveway I saw another car there, a blue Land Cruiser with a tracing of rust on the bumpers. Had the look somehow of a traveling vehicle, a practical but fun wagon. Stickers from tourist places (Trees of Mystery, Grand Canyon, etc.) on the back window. No one in the family owned a car like that. No one in my family. Or so I thought. Had she made a call?

I grabbed up my purse, camera and the sack of bread, carried them to the front door. I heard a whisper of voices from inside - I rapped lightly. Aunt Sophie didn't call to come in, I figured she couldn't hear me so I turned the knob and walked in.

"Hello? Aunt Sophie?" My heart was pounding and it irritated me. This was my Aunt's house, no strange voices should be coming from it and getting me so nervous! The front door opened onto her living room which had a couch and a couple easy chairs. There were some things on the couch, a man's jacket, a paper bag, a small suitcase. Hmmm. I went on through to the dining room, at least the room where the dining table sat. No one there. I dropped the bread onto the table. There were the voices again, a male voice, and Aunt Sophie answering him. It sounded like they were outside beyond the kitchen, through the window and the back door that were both open. I left my purse and camera on the kitchen counter and following the voices through the kitchen and out the screen door I entered onto this scene: Aunt Sophie and a man both kneeling by the flower bed just beyond the back door. He was digging a hole with a trowel, planting something? Aunt Sophie was holding a jar of water out to him as I approached, noticed by neither of them.

He laid the trowel aside and reached into a short bucket at his left, fishing for one of the plants I could see but didn't immediately recognize.

"Aunt Sophie, what'cha doing?" I said from about three feet behind them, to which they both jumped a little, water sloshing from Aunt Sophie's jar. They turned on their knees to look at me, turning inward so that their faces were side by side. I saw double. Sampson was Aunt Sophie's son, no doubt about it. The angular faces and hair the same, swept back so that the little peak at the hairline showed, her hair white, his still mostly black but with some gray streaks throughout. A little longer than the norm for men his age but full and bushy ending right at the nape of his neck. A long neck, like Aunt Sophie's.

The blue eyes of both looked at me, smiling. Comfortable with each other in the garden. The sun shined and the birds chirped.

"Oh, my." It was all I could say. They both laughed.

"You're just in time," Aunt Sophie said, gestured towards the wooden path that ran through her garden. "Annie. Set yourself down while we finish planting these wild strawberries. Sam brought them to me from home."

'Home?' I was a little jealous and unsettled by his terminology, Aunt Sophie belongs to me - this is her home. With an inner shake I sat on the lawn. They returned to their work, Aunt Sophie speaking to me, pointing with the jar to Sampson.

"Annie, meet your cousin Jonathan Sampson Smithers. Sam, this is your cousin Annie, my favorite niece."

I laughed. "She says that to all of us. 'Course she really means it with me."

"I'd shake your hand," Sampson said, in a strong but gentle voice (was I hearing an echo of David?), "but you can see, I'm busy. Mom just couldn't wait to get these in the ground."

I heard the 'Mom' and controlled a start.

"He brought them up from the cabin," Aunt Sophie said, in a voice I'd never heard edged as it was with a maternal and, yes, ownership tone. "One of the last patches left as most of it is grass now he tells me. A proper lawn." She sighed.

Sampson took the jug from her and poured the water into the cavity. He scooped up the rest of the berry plants and arranged them in the muddy row.

"Don't you have a hose around here?" he asked looking around. I jumped up to get the hose from where it was curled up at the side of the house. I turned it on to a slow stream and brought it to him. He laid it beside the row and after firming the ground around the berry plants he added water until it was overflowing.

They both leaned back from their knees and said, "There!" at the same time. We all laughed.

"Annie!" Aunt Sophie said, "Help me up!" I gave her my arm and Sampson steadied her under her other arm as I pulled her up. "Sampson!" she commanded, "That's enough water. Let's go wash up, and eat!" He got up, more easily than she, but he wasn't young, either. Just how old was he? Born around, what, 1920 wasn't it?

He rejected her outstretched hand, "Thanks, Mom. I got it." And he did. A minutes calculations reminded me that he was over 55, an old guy. It seemed odd that Aunt Sophie's baby could be old.

He was taller than she by about 6 inches. From his pants pocket he pulled a handkerchief that he wiped his hands on. Stained but cleaned of the mud he reached out to me with his right hand. "A proper hello, cousin Annie. I've heard a lot about you." Aunt Sophie busied herself rolling up the hose to put back at the side of the house, but she was attentive, threw me a little smile.

"And I've heard a lot about you!"

"I 'spect you have." He gathered up the trowel and the pad that his mother had kneeled on. He looked around for where to put them.

I was proud to be able to show him where we put the tools.

"Over here, beside the house in the little shed that Uncle Boyd built for Aunt Sophie. I opened the door to the shed. "Give me that." He handed over the trowel, the pad, and the empty water jar. "We put them here." 'We', 'our', I liked using those ownership words. And then felt silly at myself. I kept talking as I put the things on a shelf and came back out of the shed. He closed the door with the little peg-latch.

"But most of what I know about you is of you as a baby and little kid."

Aunt Sophie opened the screen door to the house, waving us in before her.

"Yes, Sam," said Aunt Sophie as she came in, starting to shut the door and then leaving it open for air, "Annie doesn't know much about you now, about what happened to you after the war."

"Oh, she doesn't want to hear all of that." He addressed me, "You don't want to hear all that." I just shrugged at him, trying to be agreeable with this stranger with whom I felt so oddly intimate. "Too long ago and too much history. Old history."

"Well, something?" I cut right to the center of my curiosity. "Are you married? Do I have little cousins? How do you make a living?" all the while thinking, I need my camera. But I let the camera lay - too intimate.

"Yes to the married, and two boys. I have pictures that I can show you after dinner. Sue and I, my wife, "he explained, "have some cottages that we run. We met at OSU." At my look of question he explained, "After the war I studied agriculture at Oregon State, but we moved back to the coast to help Mom and Dad with the running of the cabins, and, just never moved away again." He swallowed. "They're both gone now, so we do it. The boys helped," He added with a shake as if to make light and pass over the death of his parents. "Don't get me wrong, we all worked very hard for a lot of years, but we have hired help now, so I can get away," he reached out to Aunt Sophie who was just setting the stew on the table.

We pulled out the chairs and sat down at the table.

"Annie! Rye bread?" Aunt Sophie exclaimed as she passed me the plate. "How clever! Nice to have something different now and then, don't you think?" She directed the latter part of her remarks to Sampson.

"Yes, indeedy." He smiled at her and then at me. "I wondered when she was ever going to let me meet my other family."

"Jonathan," The formal reproach made us both look at her. She explained, "You surely understand, it was different times and then .. it never seemed the time to just bring you up! Oh, not you!" she was stumbling around her words, trying to smooth out the harshness. "The situation. And I wanted to protect you too." She put down the knife that she was buttering her bread with and reached out her hand to put it over his, "I couldn't stand to see any condemnation of either you or me, or your father .. so I lived with it and built a life here without you. And I wish," she added, pulling her hand away and wringing in with the other one and dropping them both into her lap, "that it could have been different. That I could have been braver. But," she got busy again with her hands, spooning stew into our bowls and handing them to us, "I wasn't."

"It's ok, Mom." He took his bowl from her.

She sighed again, this time a lighter sound, a relieved sigh, happy. She began to eat and Sampson filled the dinner with tales of his life in the years between then and now.

He had come to visit his Sophie mother after the war, which began the healing for both of them. Usually in October, after the tourist season died down, he and Sue would bring the boys up and spend a week playing in the city. After they started school he would come up by himself or they would just come up for the weekend; the boys knew her as Grandma Sophie. They never stayed at Aunt Sophie's, always staying in a hotel downtown where they invited Grandma for dinner and went together to Jantzen Beach Amusement Park. One year his sister Lily and her family spent their vacation, from Wyoming, playing with them in the amusement park. Riding the roller coaster, eating cotton candy, taking her grandchildren up in the

Ferris wheel even though it scared her to death! Sampson and Aunt Sophie especially enjoyed telling me about that weekend and I could see that somehow that had healed something in her, filled in something that she had missed more dreadfully and deeply than I could imagine.

After dinner he showed me photos, and he let me take a couple of them together, it was still light outside so I got a couple of great shots of the two of them by her new berry patch.

"Oh!" she said as we came out of the dusk back into the dim house. "I almost forgot! Turn on some lights, please, Annie. Sampson, please, the sack."

He handed her the paper bag that I'd noticed on the couch when I came through the house but hadn't thought about once I'd got outside and saw him.

"Here, hold it," she pushed the bag out to me so that I held it on the bottom while she reached in and pulled out the contents.

The quilt.

Sampson put his things on the floor and he and she stretched it out over the back of the couch, arranging it so I could see "The Beach In Winter": Haystack Rock, the Fingers, the tide pools, the ocean, the lighthouse shining through the gray sky. It was faded and ragged in places, the binding coming loose around the bottom. She fussed with it, tucking the binding into place, "Oh, you'll have to leave it with me, it needs some mending." She smoothed the edges of the pieces she'd sewed onto the material, her memories becoming tactile to me as I watched. It was more beautiful, maybe because I knew the history, than any other quilt of hers I'd seen. The work wasn't as fine as her later prizewinning ones but there was a life there in that putting together of pieces of fabric that stunned me. And of course I wanted it, but it was Sampson's. The way he handled it when he helped Aunt Sophie fold it to put it back in the bag to leave with her to mend showed me that. I did get to take a photo of her with the quilt when she had mended it, it is tucked into the corner of the mirror by the table where I write.

The photos and memories are all that I have left of her now. Let me not forget cousin Sampson! He and Sue are important to me, we are good friends as well as relatives with whom we can be honest and open.

That night after Sampson left and I was getting ready to leave, she reached for me and hugged me tighter than she ever had. We never did talk about it again. She died peacefully in her sleep some years later. I have the box, and some other things to remember her by, though I don't need any thing for that.

I thought a lot about her story, and why she told it to me, after keeping it closed within herself for all those years. Perhaps the most amazing thing of all was that after she opened her secret up with me she then told the whole family, in one fell swoop. She took him to the yearly family reunion on Memorial Day which is always held at the cemetery where my grandparents are buried. We put flowers on the graves and then picnic after at a park nearby. The open mouths of her remaining brother, Willie and sister Mandy, were a sight to see. After he closed his mouth Willie just nodded a knowing smile, and said, "Soph, I'm happy for you and, young man, welcome into the family. Long time no see," and he laughed to himself. Nobody was quite sure what he meant but it didn't matter. Great Aunt Mandy, however, was confused - some of it was natural that had come with age- but it appeared to me more (and Aunt Sophie agreed with me, later) surprised that such a thing had happened and that she had never known about it.

"Well, 'Sampson', is it?" she handed him a plate, you could see she thought this name was weird, "get yourself something to eat." She waved at the picnic table, and added, apparently as an afterthought, "Join the family." She walked away muttering, "I don't know why it was such a big secret, Sophie always had to do things her own way, never trusting us." The children of Mandy that were there, my dad and a few of his brothers and sisters, were reserved at first, feeling the way I did maybe, uncertain about our relationships, and our place now in Aunt Sophie's affections. Had the love all those years been a lie - she sure looked happier with Sampson than with us all, but again, it was the fear of being replaced, talking. That faded

179

rather quickly as we all adjusted our family roles to include a nephew, cousin who was easy going and had a family of his own that he brought the next year to the reunion.

We all started feeling pretty rich, and happy to have a family member who has cabins at the beach that we can rent for less! He didn't want to charge anything but we are not a bunch of freeloaders, but are willing to take a break if we can get it!

I stopped seeing Len soon after my weekend with Aunt Sophie. The pull to submit to him was strong, it would have been so easy. But he laughed at me once too often and during the fight told me that once we were married he didn't want me, "fooling around with that picture business anymore. I don't want a wife who smells like a chemist!"

I wasn't sure after that that I wanted to date again, but of course, I did, and now I think I've found a man who is secure enough in himself to enjoy my love of photography, knows that it's part of me.

We're going down to the beach this weekend, to the cabins, and for cousins Sampson and Sue to get a good look at him. Who knows, as we say in the trade, what might develop?

I think Aunt Sophie would like him.

The End